John F. Carr

the
OPHIDIAN
CONSPIRACY

MAJOR BOOKS • CHATSWORTH, CALIFORNIA

One

"BUT I DON'T UNDERSTAND, Spokesman," whined the Advisor. "First you suggest that I remove this Investigator, and then, when I describe the perfect means for his disposal you get angry."

No wonder we have been the minority party for over twenty-five thousand years, thought Spokesman Eral Salkow, head of the Revisionist Party and member of the Inner Council, looking at the sleeve of the Advisor's white tunic which was marked with three green bands, symbolizing that he had attained the Third Level. For the first time in its history, the Revisionist Party was close to holding a majority in the Supreme Committee, and he meant to do everything in his power to see that nothing or no one jeopardized its position.

"I want the man incapacitated, not eliminated," said the Spokesman. "Investigator Veblen is a most unusual man. He is a man of extraordinary intelligence and capability, and the youngest Investigator to hold the office. This, coupled with the fact that he is a member of neither party, makes him a most dangerous individual. We have examined every public posture and word of this man—and some private—and have reached the conclusion that his sympathies lie with the Orthodoxy. However, we cannot afford to alienate him from us by an unsuccessful murder attempt. This man is relentless and would stop at nothing to uncover his malefactors. It is for these reasons that I want him to be defanged. Is this clear?"

"Quite clear, Spokesman," answered the Advisor. "I will contact our operative and give him this information."

"Is this operative competent enough for such a delicate assignment?"

"Most discreet and very clever; in fact, you may know him. His name is. . . ."

"Don't tell me. The fewer who know him and his mission the better."

"Of course, Spokesman," replied the Advisor, his brow creased with a frown. "I will contact him at once."

"What's bothering you, Advisor," asked the Spokesman, who owed much of his tenure in office to his scrupulous attention to detail.

"I'm just wondering what will become of the Investigator's mission afterwards?"

"His assistant will take over, I imagine," answered the Spokesman curtly.

"I wonder if Vera is capable of dealing with the snake-men."

"You mean the Ophidians."

"Right, Spokesman," he stammered, "I just wonder if we can afford to loose them upon the universe again. The last time they devastated Andromeda and blackened half the Procrustean Spiral. It is said that they were as responsible for the wane of Trisaurian rule as the Invader Wang was for the damage."

"They may have been the scourge of the universe fifty thousand years ago, but things have changed since then. They no longer rule millions of slave worlds, and have but merely a few ships. There is little chance of them threatening our stability, although they might prove to be the catalyst we need to gain power."

"I don't understand how the snake-men could help our party."

"The answer lies within yourself," said the Spokesman. "At the first inkling of a threat from a race that was almost completely eradicated from the universe—or so thought to be until we rediscovered them in a planet in the Larger Magellanic Cloud, nine thousand years ago—you react as though a lost member of the Trisaurian family has returned leading an armada. Thanks to popular legend, and Solido space operas, their memory has been used to terrify misbehaving youngsters and Solido addicts for years, and has left an imprint on the public mind that's unrivaled."

"But how does that help our party?"

The Spokesman let his eyes focus on the ceiling's restful patterns for several seconds and then continued. "In our society the Ophidians have become an archetypical symbol of danger and evil. Now, if the norms and the lower levels of the professions should somehow come to believe that the Orthodoxy—through mismanagement and incompetence—has let this plague loose upon them; I believe that there would be some interesting political repercussions. Is that clear enough?"

"I see it now," answered the Advisor, "though I still feel we may be opening Pandora's box."

With advisors like this, thought the Spokesman, no

wonder the critics are claiming that Anomian society is on the decline. Which was one more reason why Orthodox rule should be brought to an end, and the Revisionists given a chance to revitalize the society and bring an end to cultural stagnation, he reasoned. "The Ophidians are not a mechanical or technological race. For even when their power was at its height, it was the humans they had enslaved who produced their warships and weapons. Their abilities lie inward, in their minds. They are keen psychologists, and the only known sentient race with proven extrasensory abilities."

"That's why I feel we should be most cautious about our dealings with them."

Superstition, the hobgoblin of mundane minds, thought the Spokesman angrily as he dismissed the Advisor with a curt wave of his hand. "Be sure and carry out my instructions to the letter."

"I will, Spokesman," said the Advisor, as he slunk towards the door.

Spokesman Salkow began to gaze upon the senscene on the far wall; a habit of his whenever he began to feel excessive anger or tension. The senscene covered the complete wall with a three-dimensional landscape which showed a small waterfall surrounded by green grass and trees, topped by an ice blue sky; not orange, crimson, green, grey, or even the purple of Anomia, but azure pure. The mural-sized senscene was one of the few remnants of Trisaurian rule, which had disappeared from Anomia over sixty-five thousand years ago. The room had once been the office of the royal Viceroy, but had long since been stripped of most of its luxurious furnishings and fancy gewgaws. The senscene was all that remained as a reminder of Imperial grandeur, though it still lent the room an opulent appearance of the earlier age.

As he watched the clear water cascade down and around the grey rocks, the Spokesman continued to brood over the possible outcomes of his decision concerning Investigator Veblen. He had tried to ferret out the man's political affiliations himself, several years earlier, and gotten nowhere. Not that Veblen, being an Investigator, was allowed to express any political bias since one of the prime qualifications for the office was political neutrality. However, that rule was rarely followed and most Investigators couldn't wait to sell their political allegiance. Veblen would be a most welcome ally but could also prove a formidable opponent, and that was a risk that he could not afford to take; not if he wanted to see the Anomian League in the hands of the Revisionist Party with himself at the helm.

The time was ripe for Revisionist rule. The worlds of the Magellanic Clouds had served as an escape valve and sanctuary for the Trisaurian Empire. The Imperial government had used these underdeveloped and unspoiled worlds as a dumping place for the adventurous and the unscrupulous, and others who did not conform to their rule. Later, when the Empire had expanded into neighboring galaxies, they exiled the fanatic and outré of every extremist political and religious group from the neo-Nazis of the Sixth Reich to the Zorastrian Triarchy to the Magellanics. This plethora of creeds and cults was allowed to nurture and propagate within the confines of the Magellanics as long as they made no attempt at intercourse with the Home Galaxy or the rest of the Empire. In this special preserve, the complete spectrum of human society flourished; each weaving its own fabric of interpersonal relations, some right out of Earth's own history and myths, others strange and bizarre. For two hundred thousand years this preserve was protected and unspoiled until the "Age of Disruption." But even during the death-throes of the Empire, the Magellanic Clouds were generally undisturbed and left to their own devices, due to their general level of primitiveness and lack of technical facilities.

Long before the sack of Orthia, capitol of the Empire, the Trisaurian Empire had withdrawn into the Home Galaxy leaving the Magellanics free to blossom and bear fruit unattended. Some twenty thousand years later, Anomia had rediscovered the hyper-drive and started its own expansion throughout the Smaller Magellanic Clouds. Under the able leadership of their sociologists, they began to spread the benefits of "scientific government" to those less able to defend themselves. Later these worlds were welded into the Anomian League and were invited to share the responsibility of rule; each planet being allowed one representative in the Supreme Committee. Some began to worry—as world after world was swallowed up by the voracious League—that the Smaller Magellanic would lose its cultural diversity, and this unparalleled collection of culture would be lost to future study.

Under the able leadership of Erhart Rohl, First Spokesman of the Orthodoxy, the idea of the Anomian Protectorate was conceived. The Protectorate was established so that these virgin cultures could continue to grow and change, free from outside intervention and contamination. On each world, Informants were placed to insure that any disturbances or violations of the Charter were reported, and to trace the study and growth of each individual society. Whenever violations occurred, they were reported by the Informants and the Investigators were called in to salvage whatever they could and to deal with the miscreants. Later, when contact was reestablished with the Larger Magellanic Cloud, this system was instituted there and opened up thousands of new worlds to sociological study. The hope being that sooner or later the "perfect" human society would germinate, and since the developmental path was unknown, all the variations of culture and behavior—even the undesirable—had to be tolerated.

There were two major opponents to the Protectorate within the League itself. The Reactionary Party, which felt that Anomia had already developed the perfect society; and the Revisionist Party, which felt that the Protectorate was an unnecessary luxury the Anomian League could no longer afford. The power vacuum in the Home Galaxy, created after the fall of the Trisaurian Empire, had been filled by a number of expansionistic and militaristic coalitions, which for the last three thousand years had been casting a hungry eye at the relatively unpolluted and untouched worlds of the Magellanic Clouds. It was only their natural distrust and suspicion of each other, and the League's navy, which had held them at bay for so long. To those living in the overcrowded Home Galaxy —filled with the fanatical, the ambitious, and the rapacious, all fighting for survival on worlds long stripped of beauty and resources—the rich and unfortified worlds of the Anomian Protectorate were indeed a tempting morsel.

A morsel that Spokesman Salkow felt was not only an invitation to trouble but a drain on the League, rather than a source of strength and economic enrichment. With the power of the People's Commonwealth increasing daily, the Esoterics building up fanatical fervor, and the Polarian Palatinate demanding new trade concessions, he knew that they could no longer afford to let these worlds continue to develop on their own and unable to contribute to the League's defense. Even with their four large and modern space fleets, they were at the mercy of any of the larger powers within the Home Galaxy.

His greatest fear was that the intricate structure of alliances and treaties that Anomia had created would break down before he had an opportunity to become First Spokesman and revitalize the League. With these many tens of thousands of worlds added to the League, they would be able to forge a wall strong enough to dissuade the most voracious invader. He had used, and would continue to use, any means at his disposal to see that the hostile forces around them would not gobble up the tiny island galaxies that formed the Magellanics.

Snapping out of his reverie, the Spokesman once again let his eyes rest on the peaceful diorama of the senscene. As he followed the tumbling water making its descent, he caught sight of a twig-like form lying on one of the flat grey rocks. He was sure he had never seen it before. After years of familiarity, he had thought that he knew every detail of the senscene's scenario and his curiosity was stimulated by this minor incongruity. Drawing closer, he saw that the object was a small black serpent drying in the light of the distant yellow sun. A sudden chill struck the base of his spine and he involuntarily shivered. Cursing himself for being a superstitious fool, he returned to his chair unable to stop his discursive mind from speculating over that inauspicious omen.

Two

FOR WHAT HAD TO BE the thousandth time, Thorstein Veblen focussed his attention on the words running past the scanner like spaceships toward the sky-dock on Anomia, while he tried to ignore the musical tones of the Heraldkey. Won't that woman ever give up, he thought to himself ruefully, as the Heraldkey once against started its song. He had assiduously managed to avoid her for the last three weeks—ever since the ship had departed from Anomia—but it didn't look as though he would be able to maintain his peace of mind much longer. Each Investigator was assigned an assistant, a Third Level Historian familiar with the background of many of the worlds which comprised the Anomian Protectorate, to help him or her complete the mission successfully. A qualified assistant was very important for the success of the mission, but just who had they assigned to him? A young woman, who, besides being an arrogant prig, was as inexperienced as himself and quite sure that she knew all the answers.

The Heraldkey began to repeat its melody again and

he popped the cassette out of the scanner and stomped over to the door. Flicking on the Ident-screen, he could see Vera Holleran's face pressed against the other side. She might even look pretty, he thought in surprise as he studied the contours of her face, if she relaxed and didn't pull her hair against her head so tightly. This thought quickly submerged beneath his mounting irritation and he hit the button that released the door.

Even before the door had finished sliding open, a torrent of words assaulted his ears. There were several slights against his manhood and lack of fertility, and a few others about the lack or absence of his intelligence before he hit the button, closing the door again.

After positioning her body so that she blocked the door's path, Vera called out, "All right, Thor, I'll behave."

"Don't call me Thor," cried Veblen indignantly. "The name is Thorstein. That is the name I chose at the Naming Ceremony and that is the way I like it said."

"Right, Thor," said Vera flippantly, "you named yourself after a twentieth century Earth sociologist, but I bet they called him Thor too."

Veblen was somewhat taken aback by this revelation, and figured that she either knew her Pre-Atomic Earth History better than most or had done some diligent research since they had been given their assignments. The original Thorstein Veblen hadn't really been a proper sociologist and he had run into some difficulty from the Naming Rules Committee— in general a rather conservative group—in obtaining permission to use the name. He, however, had been impressed by the scope of the original Veblen's erudition and accomplishments, which included important contributions to the fields of history, philosophy, economics, as well as sociology. Besides his renaissance reach of mind, the original Thorstein Veblen had shown talent as a keen social critic and an impassive observer and chronicler of the human condition.

"Holy Sanity," cried Vera, as she edged past him. "This room is really a mess. No wonder you've been afraid to let anyone in here."

Veblen groaned loudly and then cleared off the cassettes and tunics which covered the small cabin's contour seat. As she sat down, he asked, "Now would you please tell me what you want that is so important that you were forced to try and beat down my door?"

For a moment her eyes sparkled dangerously and then she sighed loudly and said, "You have just got to be one of the most exasperating men alive!"

"Humph," he returned, rather than voicing several thoughts that were better left unsaid.

"The two of us have been assigned together to work as a team," she continued, "and to be quite honest, I'm no happier about the idea of working with you than you are about working with me."

Well, of course, he thought to himself, it was obvious that she had been assigned to him for political reasons. The Revisionist Party had worked hard to try to block his nomination to the vacated Investigator's post; and in an attempt to appease the opposition, the selection committee had appointed an assistant with well-known Revisionist leanings and ties. He wondered, cynically, how that was supposed to help their mission.

"And furthermore," continued Vera, "I don't even know how I'm going to help you, since I don't even know what our assignment is all about. Don't you think it's about time you let me know?"

Well, she had a legitimate point, he thought begrudgingly, as he was well aware that he preferred to work by himself. So he twisted his face into what he thought was a congenial smile and said, "What is it that you would like to know?"

"First of all, I'd like to know our destination."

"We are headed for the planet Seker. You are familiar with it?"

"Of course," she said eagerly. "That is the planet which was settled by the Ophidian survivors of the 'Great Search,' after the Trisaurian Emperor Nicholas XIII called an Imperial Crusade against them."

"He had good reason," said Veblen. "If left unchecked, the Ophidians or snake-men, as they are commonly called, would have wrested control of this part of the universe from the hands of man. For when Nicholas called his crusade, the Ophidians had established their dominance over the spiral of Orion, Andromeda, along with several other galaxies. They were beginning to threaten the Home Galaxy itself. On every world they controlled, the human population was enslaved and, while they were for the most part well treated, they were at the total mercy of their alien overlords."

"While most of what you have just said is substantially correct," said Vera, with a gleam in her eyes, "it is now a proven fact that the Ophidians are not aliens but of human stock."

"The hell you say," ejected Veblen, somewhat taken aback.

"H. G. Wells, probably the most eminent historian of our age, has just recorded a tract intitled, *The Origins of the Ophidian Oligarchy.* In this tract—which contains a wealth of material never before available and obtained directly from the Institute of Intergalactic History on Terra—Wells proves that the Ophidians were bio-formed during the reign of Alexis the Mad, who had ordered the creation of an elite bodyguard which would owe him complete loyalty. His genetic engineers experimented with human and snake chromosomes until they had created a being which, they felt, combined many of the best features of both species. The Ophidians, the end product of their experiments, were endowed with high intelligence, very quick reflexes, the ability to function in almost total darkness, a high degree of psychic sensitivity, and strong control over their emotions. The Ophidians proved to be almost perfect bodyguards, and during Alexis' rule—which was marked by a number of rebellions and uprisings—they managed to save his life several times, proving to be both incorruptible and deadly. In one of his more expansive moods he rewarded them, after a particularly close attempt on his life—not at all that uncommon during the Age of Disruption—with a number of Imperial cruisers and several square parsecs of territory in the core of the Andromeda Galaxy. This territory formed the base of their later conquests, and the center of their political administration.

"Their human origin is further substantiated by Wells' discovery that the Ophidian's clan and tribal names are nearly identical to the generic names given to those snakes indigenous to the planet Terra. This evidence, when combined with recent genetic findings, he feels, proves conclusively that the Ophidians are an offshoot of the human race."

"Humph," repeated Veblen, impressed by his new colleague but not about to let her know it. "It's too bad they didn't assign me Wells, he might have proven to be a real asset on this mission. He saw a flash of pain in her eyes and felt a momentary stab of guilt which he covered by saying, "Well, do you have any more questions?"

Vera shot him a reproachful look. "Yes. Would it be asking too much for you to tell me what this assignment is all about?"

"Not at all. The Bureau recently learned, from one of our Informants on Seker, that the Ophidians have just obtained several interplanetary spacecraft from an unknown source. Someone is responsible for a flagrant violation of the League's Charter, and it is our job to find out who and to stop them before irreparable damage has been done to the Ophidians' society and its institutions."

"Is it possible that the Ophidians built the ships themselves?" asked Vera.

Veblen lifted his eyebrows and said, "I'm surprised, I thought you knew everything there was to know about the Ophidians. They may be gifted with psychic abilities and photo-sensitivity, but they are completely lacking in any mechanical talent or ability. Their lack of mechanical aptitude was the major reason that the Ophidian Oligarchy found it necessary to enslave human beings. Finding themselves unable to produce the interstellar spaceships, weapons, and other technological hardware they needed, the Ophidians found it more profitable to subjugate human worlds, and use their subject population, than to trade with the ravenous merchants of the time—who weren't much different than the Symbonesse traders of today. Therefore, there is no doubt that someone or some group brought those ships to Seker."

"Oh," said Vera curtly. "Are there any clues as to where the ships might have come from?"

"No. Unfortunately, the Informant who was involved received his information secondhand and was unable to see the ships themselves. Only a select circle have been allowed to see them, and none of them to my knowledge has been human."

"You mean there are humans on Seker too?"

"Of course! You didn't know?"

"I'm an historian not a sociologist," said Vera frostily.

"After the fall of the Ophidian Oligarchy," began Veblen, obviously enjoying his role of teacher, "as I'm sure you're well aware," he added as an aside, "the Ophidians—that is, those who weren't murdered by their former slaves and underlings—tried to flee from the Imperial fleet. Those who escaped the battles of Sirax III, the Antar Nebula, and the Lobo Trail were hunted down by packs of Imperial dreadnoughts, until Emperor Nicholas was satisfied that they had all been destroyed. It wasn't until about nine thousand years ago, after the exhaustive exploration of the Larger Magellanic Cloud had been almost concluded, that the existence of the Ophidians was discovered and it was decided that several of the Ophidian ships had managed to elude the Emperor's dragnet."

"I thought you were going to tell me something I didn't already know," interrupted Vera.

Ignoring her, Veblen continued. "It almost goes without saying that the overnight disappearance of a once-mighty people is almost without parallel in the annals of history."

"That's not true," interjected Vera, "the Assyrians, a Pre-Industrial Earth people, invaded the fertile cresent of Mesopotamia and built an empire that included most of the world including Egypt and Babylonia. The Assyrians were a military race and

19

were infamous for the cruelty and severity of their reign. However, their barbarity and savagery did not go unavenged; when their subject populations revolted, they literally decimated their former masters."

"Anyway, as I was saying," snapped Veblen, giving her a scowl. "The Ophidians brought with them the things they felt were most important for continued survival, including a significant number of their human slaves.

"They're not still using humans as slaves, are they?"

"Yes," answered Veblen. "It is one of the Protectorate's basic policies to never interfere with the customs, folkways, mores, morals, laws, and institutions of any of the worlds within its jurisdiction. No one, not even we sociologists, have any absolute knowledge about what elements are needed for the creation of the ideal human society. If we were to try and force our own morality and ethics upon these evolving societies, we would only produce stale variations of our own cultural theme. As scientists, we have to rise above ordinary moral and legal perspectives and judge these societies on their own individual merit and accomplishments, not on their similarity to our own ethnocentric prejudices."

"I should think it is our duty," replied Vera angrily, "to use our advanced knowledge and learning to enlighten and elevate those who are less fortunate—instead of condemning them to a life of darkness and ignorance."

Clasping his hands tightly in frustration, Veblen said: "Wait until you've been on a few of these worlds before you begin to jump to unwarranted conclusions and stifle your intelligence behind stale clichés and muddled thinking."

Vera's face began to redden. "And I suppose you approve of slavery?"

"Not particularly," answered Veblen, "though I'm convinced that we are all slaves of one thing or another: ignorance, convention, morality, and our own misconceptions. The kinds of slavery are as numerous as those of freedom, and the Ophidian kind is one of the more tolerable. As we shall soon both find out."

"What do you mean?"

"You didn't think that we were going to pass as Ophidians, did you?"

"No. . . ."

"Good. I wouldn't want to surprise you at this late date, since we're both going to sample Ophidian slavery firsthand."

"You don't mean that someone is going to *own* me," cried Vera, her face turning white.

"Not exactly. Though there is still some personal slavery on Seker, but to be owned would cut down our mobility. For while every human on Seker is a slave, after sixty thousand years, it has gone through many changes."

"Like what?"

"On Seker, the humans and Ophidians have developed an almost symbiotic relationship wherein the humans have taken over many of the social and economic tasks, which the Ophidians either have no aptitude for or any interest in doing. So instead of being the slaves of individual Ophidians, many humans have become the property of a clan or tribe to which they pay a yearly head tax for the privilege of unrestricted movement and employment. This is not a far cry from the income and personal taxes of many so-called free societies."

"What you're really saying is that the humans do all the hard labor while the Ophidians revel in a drone-like existence."

"No, that is not what I'm saying," said Veblen. "The Colubrinae and Boidae clans do the majority of the menial tasks, including some which the humans are quite capable of doing. Of course, many humans are laborers and workers, but the majority perform tasks that the Ophidians won't or can't, such as mechanical and engineering work. Furthermore, since most Ophidians despise usury and mercantilism, humans control most of the economic enterprise on Seker. As a result, many of the wealthiest and most powerful individuals, though not in a political or social sense, are humans. However, you'll understand it all much better after the Intercortical RNA Memory Transfer has been completed, then you will have an unique grasp of slavery and human and Ophidian relationships."

Seeing a look of consternation across her face, he paused, and then said, "You didn't think we were going to make a memory transfer with an Ophidian, did you? The majority of physiopsychologists feel that only a person with a very strong sense of personal identity would be able to survive such a memory transfer, and still retain their sanity. The influx of alien, or nonhuman thought and perspective, would put an enormous strain upon the subject's sense of identity and psychological integration. However, since the Ophidian and human chromosomal nucleotides are compatible, theoretically such a memory transfer is possible, but. . . ."

Veblen stopped as he caught a glimpse of anxiety in Vera's eyes, and frightening insight popped into his mind. "You've never had a memory transfer before, have you!" he cried accusingly.

As she turned away from his inquisitive eyes, he heard a faint "no" in answer to his question. He dropped his face into his hands and began to moan.

"It's not my fault," she said. "I hadn't finished my training course before our appointments were made. As you know, my appointment was rather hasty."

Another ill-conceived political abortion, thought Veblen bitterly, and he wondered what had happened to those with better preparation but poorer political affiliation. "Do you have even the slightest idea of the psychological confusion and disorder that occurs when a completely new and different mental matrix is suddenly let loose in your mind. No, of course, you don't. It's something that has to be experienced to be understood."

"If you could survive it," she replied stiffly, "I'm sure that I can too."

"I hope so," said Veblen frowning, "because I'm going to need all the help I can get on this assignment. I've seen many reactions to an Intercortical RNA Memory Transfer—from quivering hebephrenia to catalepsy. There is no way, in advance of the transfer, of foreseeing how a mind will react to the sudden influx of foreign ribonucleic acid and the memories and thought patterns it contains. A whole new frame of reference will be resurrected inside your skull. Although this transferred personality matrix doesn't have a will of its own, it will reflexively try to reorder incoming data and perceptions around it into perceivable and orderly patterns as it understands them."

"Can this revived personality take over its host?" asked Vera nervously.

"Impossible," said Veblen sharply. "That is just another fallacy propagated by moronic Solido melodramas. A personality is more than the sum of its RNA memory codes; there are neural and electrical pathways particular to each individual brain, as well as distinctive endocrine balances and inputs. The mind is not localized in any one subsystem but is an overall phenomenon comprised of several systems. There does not exist one true recorded case of personality possession after a memory transfer—though there are records of some minds which have acted as though such a possession had occurred. However, despite popular prejudices to the contrary, these have usually proven to be cases of latent paranoia or schizophrenia which were precipitated by the sudden inclusion of foreign thought patterns and memories."

"We still have a couple of weeks before we reach Seker," said Vera. "Couldn't I use hypno-tapes and memory amplifiers to learn the language?"

If there would have been any possible way, Veblen would have dropped the case right then and there. Trying to contain his rising anger, he said slowly and deliberately, "As Investigators, we have neither the time nor the inclination to involve ourselves in long-term learning operations. It is nonproductive. An Investigator's job is to land on a problem planet, locate the difficulty, solve it, and leave. All with as little disturbance to the culture and its people as possible. The memory transfer makes it possible for the Investigator to speak the language and know the customary social behavior patterns without wasting any time or effort in their mastery. A side benefit of the memory transfer is that unless they are reinforced, both the language and behavioral patterns will fade from the memory within a year or two. Therefore the Investigator is able to arrive at an unknown planet, become—for all practical purposes—

a member of that society, solve the problem, and leave; all without any permanent retention of useless language and customs to encumber him in the future."

"So then I really don't have any choice," Vera said, shrugging her shoulders.

"No," answered Veblen. "And for both our sakes, I hope you don't experience any adverse side effects."

Vera nodded her head glumly in agreement.

Three

AS HIS FEET PASSED over the smooth-worn stones below, Magus Avanar, of the Micrurus tribe, mentally exorcised the tiny fireball of anger he felt within himself and placed it in the air before him. While it hung there suspended in mid-air, he used his powers of concentration to turn the illusionary ball of fire into a shower of blue-white sparks. The tiny pinpoints of light were swallowed by the blackness around him and he felt an oceanic wave of peace and tranquility wash through the corridors of his mind, and a benign smile awoke within and without. He hadn't felt an emotion this strong since he had been an acolyte at the university, and he felt a momentary longing for that beloved sanctuary. Treacherous emotion and disquietude was the price he payed for traffic with the outside world.

Curiosity as to how much farther he had to walk down the darkened hallway caused him to dilate his elliptical pupils, until he caught the faint glow from the taper set next to the door at the end of the hall. He couldn't help but think that this darkened corridor would be the ideal place for an assassination attempt by the Mambas, a secret sect devoted to murder and demonic ceremony. It was doubtful that one of their minions would have been able to work his way past several watches of guards and into the Council Hall's inner sanctum; though they had been known, in the past, to even violate the sacred neutrality of the Hatchery in order to consummate one of their nefarious crimes. He flicked his forked tongue in and out several times to test the damp air and he received the smell/taste of several sensations; the wet grit of moist stone, the acrid/sweet smoke of burnt oil, and the still-pungent wisps of snake scent now several hours old. The heat-receptors concentrated beneath his forehead felt no other warmth than that of the approaching light and he was aware that his worries were unnecessary; but he quickened his pace anyway.

In recent days strange rumors and guarded insinuations had whisked through the narrow streets and alleys of Buzthara, and it was one such that had brought him to the First Elder's chamber in such a hurry. After his many years of study and meditation within the cloistered halls of the university, this tense mood now hanging over the city had frightened him. Maybe the Brethren had concentrated too much of their energy upon their lofty goals and ideals and had lost touch with those they sought to help. He was openly amazed at the terror and fascination the old superstitions still exerted over the citizenry of the world's major city. Recently, several prominent Ophidians had disappeared and a number of human corpses had surfaced. The bodies had been found headless and with the entrails removed; a salient reminder of ancient augury unforgotten and still practiced in secret. He wondered what role the off-worlders played in this drama and why the First Elder's ominous silence.

Reaching the door he rang the small bell of green-stained brass four times, as was required, and waited for permission to enter. After the words of invitation had been chanted, and the proper time had elapsed, he opened the door and walked into the chamber. He tried to ignore the pain in his eyes caused by the flood of light issuing forth from the two tapers, one set on either side of the room. The First Elder was seated in a large wooden chair which had sacred runes carved into its armrests and backboard. He was dressed in the dark blue robes of the Viperidae Clan and wore the white olynx skin cloak of office, fastened by a silver clasp with the Cerastes tribal emblem, the crocodile, emblazoned upon it.

As Avanar approached the Elder, the other man set aside his staff of office and came to his feet beginning the first movements of the greeting ritual. His head darted back and forth, the Elder slowly approached with his arms extended and his palms down. Avanar performed the same movements until their hands almost touched, then he sank down until he was resting on one knee with his head bent forward almost touching the ground. When this part of the ceremony was completed, the Elder drew back, motioning with his hands for his guest to return to his feet. Standing once more, Avanar folded his arms across his chest and then sat down. When the greeting ritual was completed, they began the identification ceremony and the Elder began to recite the names of his tribal forefathers. After he had finished, Avanar reciprocated until he had covered twenty generations of his ancestors.

"It has been a long time since we have met outside the Council meetings," stated the Elder. "Would I be right in assuming that this is not a social call?"

"That is a correct assumption," replied Avanar gravely. "I have come to validate a rumor I have heard concerning the off-worlders."

"I had not thought you one who would bend so low as to hear the city's lower rumblings."

"A truly open mind examines all, even that which had been eliminated."

The First Elder smiled and said, "What have you heard Master Magus, that not only has sharpened your expression but your wit as well?"

"It has been whispered that you have offered those off-worlders a refuge without having consulted the Council first. The Council gave you permission to receive several spacecraft as gifts—against my, and others', council—from the off-worlders; but there was no mention of future compensation."

"The Council is wise and learned, but there are times when the fast current of events requires a single swimmer; or why else would there be a First Elder. The off-worlders have offered to help us restore that which was once rightfully ours, and I have snatched their offer in haste lest the time of debate and consideration leave it stillborn and our destiny forfeit."

"Why would the off-worlders want to help us take what their ancestors fought long and hard to wrest from ours?"

"The overlords of the worlds of men change like broken teeth, and those which grow back have little memory of those who rested there before, and the blows that fractured them. These men request an alliance to help them break the chains of those who bind us to this world and many others like us."

"Why should we help them destroy those who over-see us, for they do us no ill. They conduct their studies in seeming secrecy and interfere not with our laws or decrees."

"They offend us with their spies," said the First Elder, his eyes sparking with anger. Surely a dangerous trait in one who rules, thought Avanar to himself. "They are only students of life," answered the Magus.

"They are our foes," returned the First Elder. "They could help restore our greatness, yet refuse."

"And what did our Empire bring us; wisdom, knowledge, truth, or enlightenment? No, little but vainglory, arrogance, pride, and stupidity; much of which is still with us, I'm afraid."

"Are you insinuating that I am arrogant and stupid," cried the First Elder, his face deathly pale. "Because if you are. . . ."

Avanar silenced the other man with his hand saying, "Think before you make any challenge that would only make both of us look foolish. Neither of us has the smooth skin of youth or even middle-age and nothing looks more ridiculous than two ancients puffing and snorting around the circle, making successively slower stabs until they both drop from fatigue."

The First Elder swallowed several times and then nodded his head in agreement.

"Now," continued Avanar, "why do these off-worlders require our aid when it is obvious that our power is but a shadow of its former substance."

"They tell me that our name is still held in fear on the worlds of man, and that many would flee before our fighting ships."

Magus Avanar shook his head sadly. "I had hoped that the infamy of our past deeds would be forgotten, and that in time the gates of the universe would be opened with welcome—not hatred."

"Why should the feelings of humans concern us! After all, are their emotions any different from the winds above? They blow with uneven strength and little predictability. One moment they are puffed out like a storm all out of control, full of sound and fury, and the next they are weeping and sobbing, their anger spent and their mood subdued."

"You are wrong, Elder. Those are the thoughts of the past. Humans have the same hopes and fears that we do, though they feel them with more intensity. It is not up to you or me to decide which is better. Our future lies in a partnership with them, for they complement us as we do them. In the past, we used their tools and weapons to forge our empire, and lost it because we did not treat them with respect and brotherhood."

"Respect!" spat the First Elder. "I will die before I give my respect to one of that inferior ilk. They are not fit to be our equals—only our slaves, as these off-worlders will find when they are no longer of any use."

"It was this kind of blind prejudice that almost ended our people's existence," said Avanar, not sure whether he should pity or loathe the other. "We must learn from our mistakes not repeat them."

"*You* are wrong," snapped the Elder. "We were too easy on them, but that mistake will not be repeated in the future. The humans are a lower form of life who best understand pain and misery."

"You don't know what you are talking about, Elder," returned the Master Magus. "At the university we have studied their anatomy and ours, and come to the conclusion that our races are closely related if not separate shoots off the same branch."

"Heresy!" screamed the First Elder, his face contorted with anger. "The body is a holy temple and dissection is forbidden by the Great Book."

"Dissection is no longer a legal crime, only a religious one," said Avanar, "as you would know if you spent more time studying the laws instead of disobeying them."

"What . . . ," sputtered the Elder, whose face started to mottle.

"It appears that you have no more emotional control than the humans you despise," observed Avanar.

"Human-lover!" cried the Elder, making it sound like a curse.

"There are worse things," answered Avanar, giving the Elder a pointed stare.

"Traitors like you will receive your proper punishment," screamed the Elder, as he began to clutch at his chest. In between coughs, the Elder threatened: "When the Oligarchy returns, I promise you a most horrible end."

Avanar laughed. "I'm afraid if you don't watch yourself, you'll never live to see it."

The Elder sat speechless, his mouth taking in deep gulps of air so that the skin around his throat was puffed out like that of some deep-water fish. However his eyes threw out twin beams of pure hatred that held more evil promise that any mere words could relay.

Magus smiled under the scathing glare. "I must warn you, Elder, that I am calling a special meeting of the Elder Council and every move you have made, independent of our authority, will come under the closest scrutiny." Magus Avanar then bowed twice and turned, ignoring the remaining ritual, and began to walk out of the chamber.

He heard the Elder continue to sputter behind him and decided that he would not leave the university again without several guards to accompany him.

Four

"I DON'T SEE WHY YOU'RE so upset," snapped Vera, as she and Veblen walked down the metal corridor towards the passengers' dining area. "You haven't once accepted the Captain's invitation to dine at his table since the voyage began, and I really don't think that it's asking too much for you to attend now."

"I'm sure he doesn't want me at his table," replied Veblen, "any more than I want to be there. Besides, I have more important things to do than to waste my time socializing."

"Well," answered Vera, "it's traditional for passengers to dine at the Captain's table after the hyperdrive shift has been successfully completed. And who knows, we might learn something."

"Humph," was Veblen's answer as they entered the elegant dining room. Three-dimensional murals covered the walls giving the room a spacious look; although closer inspection showed that the area was no larger than absolutely necessary. The Captain was seated at the head of the table and Veblen was sure that the older man had given him a scowl as he entered. The steward sat them to the Captain's right, a place of honor, in accordance with the Investigator's high status. They were the last to arrive and Veblen felt uncomfortable under the combined stares of the other passengers. This being his first appearance, the Captain introduced him to his fellow travellers. He was surprised at the heterogeneous makeup of the ship's company; two dour-looking Commissars from the People's League, an overdressed elderly woman from the planet Xersat, a purple-robed Brother from the Esoterics, and the Dauphin of Nice and his retinue.

"That is everyone but . . . ," commented the Captain, who came to a stop as a tall lanky man with a gnome-like face walked into the dining room. He was dressed simply in a black caftan, devoid of design as well as any identifying marks. The man's face was blank but his eyes were as deep as the space surrounding the ship, and his appearance had a quieting effect on the ship's company. The Captain identified him simply as Mordicai; no surname, no star system.

"That's the first time I've seen him," whispered Vera, as the man sat solemnly down. "Do you know who he is, Thor?"

Veblen winced and said, "From his appearance I'd guess that he's a member of the Terran Illuminati, a secret society rumored to have been started on Earth during the Pre-Atomic Age."

"But that's almost three hundred and eighty thousand years ago!"

"Hold it down," answered Veblen under his breath. "I know, I'm skeptical about that myself. Anyway, the society is said to have its base on a rogue planet named Eris. The membership is quite small and they are dedicated to the rise of discord and the decline of civilization throughout the universe. Their motto goes like this: 'When war flames, chaos reigns.' "

"How awful," she replied in a hushed tone. "I wonder why I've never run across any mention of them in my studies."

"There's very little mention of them in any of the major references," said Veblen, "and I didn't even really believe in their existence myself until he walked into this room."

"Do you think they may be involved in the trouble on Seker?"

"No," he whispered. "It's too organized to be an Illuminati conspiracy."

They both quieted as Brother Vomisa began grace. The Brotherhood of the Order of Universal Symmetry was a relatively new religion when contrasted to Christianity, Buddhism, Mithraism, Doreism, and other religions. However, it was by far the fastest growing and most powerful religion in the Home Galaxy, and its converts were zealously spreading its word throughout the worlds of man. Its major creed was that man can only attain godlike grace in this life, and the hereafter, when he has removed disorder and irrationality from his life and person. Order, symmetry, and efficiency were the Holy Trinity and it was a true believer's sacred duty to spread the word and convert the heathen. To the Order of Universal Symmetry, the man and machine integration was the next step in the escalade to godhood; and the cyborg the ultimate in the man-machine interface. The Brotherhood did not believe in the separation of state and church, and had established its religious theocracy in a quadrant of the Home Galaxy that was commonly called the Esoterics.

When the Brother's litany came to a welcome end,

and the steward began to serve the wine, Veblen noticed that alcohol was one form of disorder not proscribed by the Brotherhood.

"Investigator," asked one of the Commissars, "are you at liberty to tell us where we are stopping."

"I'm sorry, Commissar," answered Veblen, "but that is classified information."

"So you're the one," cried the Dauphin, his hand limply beating the air in Veblen's direction. "By what right have you had this ship's course changed? This little escapade of yours is costing me a considerable delay from my palace in Nice. It is simply intolerable."

"I'm sorry about the inconvenience, Dauphin," returned Veblen sarcastically, "but in Anomia the good of the majority is held above that of the individual. All goods and services are owned in common and a mission of state is considered to have priority over the convenience of a few travellers." He felt Vera's elbow slicing into his ribs and a few choice comments on being diplomatic whispered into his ear.

"Horrible," cringed the Dauphin. "On Nice, the value of the aristocracy, and the guidance it provides, is appreciated by those of lesser birth."

"One of these days," interjected one of the Commissars, "you and your corrupt cronies will receive your just rewards."

"Well, I never!" minced the Dauphin.

The argument was interrupted by the arrival of dinner and Veblen gave a silent sigh of relief. And people wondered why he preferred to eat alone in his cabin. Whatever the calibre of the company, the first course proved to be excellent.

"What exactly does an Investigator do," the Commissar asked as they waited for the next course.

"In essence," answered Veblen, "our job is to see that there is no unnecessary interference with the cultural and technological development on any of the worlds protected by the Protectorate's Charter. Whenever any disruption of the normal pattern takes place, we are contacted and it's our job to rectify the situation."

"It sounds as though it could get dangerous."

"At times."

"You're not planning on taking Vera into any danger," cried the Dauphin.

He tried to hide the annoyance he felt by the Dauphin's use of Vera's first name and answered curtly: "I'm sure she's just as capable of taking care of herself as any one of us."

"What a barbarous attitude," sniffed the Dauphin.

Vera made a feline smile of contentment and added pointedly, "Dauphin, I'm afraid that the men of Anomia don't have either the manners or sensitivity one grows accustomed to in the older and wealthier Core worlds."

"I suppose that's the price one must pay for living out here in the frontier," he answered, his nostrils flaring in distaste.

Veblen returned his attentions to the fillet that graced the plate before him, trying his best to ignore the animated conversation between Vera and the Dauphin on the relative merits of this year's fashions. As his knife sliced through the meat with ease, he wondered whether it was synthetic or real; it was difficult to tell the yeast and oil-based proteins from the flesh they imitated. He didn't doubt that in another ten thousand years or more, people would look upon those who ate real meat as cannibals or worse.

In spite of the good meal in front of him, Veblen

felt a growing irritation as the tête à tête continued between Vera and the aristocratic fop sitting next to her. Why that should bother him caused him considerable additional agitation, and in desperation he began to talk to the Brother sitting across from him at the table. "It's most unusual to see a member of your order within the boundaries of the League; are you here on business?"

"In a manner of speaking," said the Brother. "I was visiting a number of your worlds as part of my survey work. As I'm sure you're aware, the Brotherhood likes to do its best to keep our census figures up to date."

The Centennial Census of the Brotherhood was well known and a basic reference in all libraries; though Veblen had often wondered whether the reason for its existence was more political than for the welfare of mankind, as the Brotherhood claimed. For the martial arm of the Brotherhood was as integral a part of their enlightenment campaign as was their spiritual arm.

"After all," continued the Brother, with a beatific smile, "the Anomian League has continually declined our offers of religious instruction."

"Prohibited might be a better word," rejoined Veblen.

"Touché," answered the Brother, a hard glare in his eyes. "One of these days you will appreciate and understand the gifts we offer to mankind. You appear to be an intelligent man and I'm surprised that you haven't taken a much closer look at our religion. For without order, all is meaningless and we are the universe's first line of defense against the forces of entrophy and chaos."

"Not interested," said Veblen. "I don't intend to

cohabit my body with any mechanical devices like one of your Proctors."

"Pure prejudice," said the Brother. "Man is limited only by his rejection of the man-machine integration. This melding of inorganic to organic is the highest reward our church has to offer, and though many desire it few are chosen. It is my fondest dream that some day I will be seleceted by the Prime Monitor as one of those fit for computer implantation. To lose the corrupting acid of emotion and to gain the cold-steel precision of logic in return—is that not the most man can ask for?"

Veblen felt a chill begin at the base of his spine. "To become a machine is to lose humanity."

"And what does humanity have to offer?" the Brother responded scornfully. "The confusion and disorder of emotion, the stupidity and frustration of frail brain tissue, or the pleasure and enjoyment of death. We of the Order of Universal Symmetry have conquered emotion, ended ignorance, and eliminated death. We have become the perfect overseers of the universe."

"Undertakers might be a better word."

"And your silly Protectorate is any more fit?"

"Maybe," answered Veblen. "At least, we aren't taking the latest cosmic truth and shoving it down anyone's throat."

The Brother's face momentarily matched the color of his purple robes, then he regained his composure. "Your society is very foolish to allow these rich worlds to lie fallow. Instead of becoming a strength, they have become a weakness as you indulge yourselves in this quixotic search for the perfect society."

"I agree," blurted the Captain, obviously in his cups.

"Ah-ha!" cried the Brother gleefully. "Then you agree that the perfect society has already appeared under the cloak of Universal Symmetry."

The Captain screwed up his face and quickly drained his wine glass signalling the steward for another. "Bunk. I just agreed with the point you made about ignoring the industrial potential of most of the Magellanic Worlds. Instead of protecting them, we are just saving them for someone else's benefit."

Another Revisionist, thought Veblen wearily, as he tried to ignore the growing debate between the Captain and Brother Vomisa. He turned his head away only to be faced with the Dauphin, who in his affected manner, was trying to act out a part in some new drama with Vera looking on avidly. Women, he growled to himself as he pushed his plate to the side and began to stand up.

"Where are you going," asked Vera.

"To my cabin," he answered, pointing toward the general clamor. "I've got a headache."

"Too bad," returned Vera, already back to her conversation with the Dauphin on the relative merits of Erik Landau, the latest Solido rave.

Five

THIS IS THE DAY OF Passover, he thought, as the cart bumped along the dusty street throwing him against his crèche brothers. They were all travelling to the Hall of Judgment to be examined by the Clan Elders, and judged to be eligible for their Tribal Totem and their rights as a Clan Novice. By tonight I will either have my true name, or be floating face down on the River Wynn. He took a long look at the stone ceiling overhead, which shed its dusty yellow glow over the wood and brick buildings that lined the street, and felt the corrosive emotion ebb. His tranquility restored, he then flicked his forked tongue in and out of its pocket, set in the roof of his mouth. The spicy air of the city was so much more alive and rich than the vapid air of the crèche, where, until today, he had spent the first ten years of his life. A loathsome smell/taste, the like of which he had never experienced, forced him back from the edge of the cart, and his eyes darted quickly over to the side of the street to identify its odious origin. He located its source and stared in amazement. The creature had a shock of brown bristles sticking from its head, a pasty white face, and an open mouth that revealed a slug-like tongue lacking in all grace and symmetry. Yet, all this was nothing when compared to the effluvium the being radiated into the air like poisonous vapors. "What sort of creature is that," he asked the Caretaker.

"A human being," the Caretaker answered. "An unnatural beast who was cursed by the Great Serpent for bearing its young live, like an insect or food animal. To punish their arrogance, the Great Serpent divided their minds and their bodies so that the two are in constant conflict. This is why the humans have so little control over what they do and how they act."

Arnth felt the club slam into his left shoulder leaving it numb and broken. Something was wrong. The club was a meter-long shaft of hard wood, with a head made of wrapped cloth; it was not made to kill but to stun. He moved back quickly and turned to favor his right side. Using his club as a shield, he tried to keep the blows raining down upon him away from his vulnerable flesh. He looked up into the seats ringing the Pit and saw the lithe form of Sandri, her emerald skin glowing in the faint light. The press of sharp stones against his bare back brought his mind back to the Pit. Any moment now, his creaking club would splinter or be knocked away and he would never know the cool/warmth of her body. A glancing blow to the side of his head brought a sense of heightened awareness, and time seemed to run like molten glass. Maybe he could survive the mating combat and live to do the mating dance. As his opponent drew back for the final coup, he darted down, grabbed a handful of sand and threw it in his face. A rumble of displeasure from the stands greeted his unforgivable break from the combat ritual. However. Arnth's bodily instincts, less shackled by custom and duty, moved his limbs to the primal dance of survival and the tip of his club punched the knot of nerves in the pit of the other's stomach. His opponent collapsed to the ground in a spasm of coughing; his black face the color of grey slate. Holding the captured club high above his head, like a trophy, Arnth exposed its metal core before the watching multitude, and was washed to one side as they poured into the Pit. Through a red haze, he watched as his former adversary was torn to pieces by the maddened mob, who righteously extracted the ages' old penalty for a violation of the Law.

A taper set into the granite wall above Arnth's head cast a red glow over the altar and the stone idol, which waited behind ready to strike. He heard the priests' voice echo through the chamber as they began the opening incantation in the Old Tongue. The idol's sharp, silver fangs pulsed blood-red in the low light, and its purple sapphire eyes seemed to gleam in anticipation. Tonight Arnth participated in his first service in the underground Temple of Raal. It was a great honor to be present at the secret and illegal ceremonies of the Mambas, and he felt proud that he had been chosen. A priest, bent over with age, stood before the idol of coiled stone, said a short prayer, and lit the incense held in a wrought iron brazier. He shivered when a shrill scream started and then was suddenly cut off. Four black-robed priests, with their hoods drawn, walked to the four corners of the altar. Then the human sacrifice was led up to the front of the chamber and laid out on the altar. The priests shackled the writhing prisoner with iron manacles so that he was held firmly. Arnth felt hatred and revulsion burn through his veins as he watched the shivering human. One day the true Ophidians would rise up in wrath, and bathe Seker with the blood of the vile humans and their degenerate protectors. His anger turned to pleasure as the sharp blade slashed through the thin white flesh spurting warm fluid into the gleaming chalices that were held beneath each of the four cuts. The salty, warm fluid soothed a thirst far more intense than any bodily need. Then his voice joined the chorus imploring Raal, God of War and Valor, to show them the sign; the signal that would herald the end of human rule throughout the universe.

The sun burned blood-red as it started its journey across the purple heaven above. Arnth squinted and then turned to face the eating humans who were chattering gaily like their simian cousins. Inside he seethed with anger and cursed the regulations that prohibited the mistreatment of human labor. His tour of outside duty was almost over, and he couldn't wait to return to the cool depths of Buzthara where it was the humans who were in the minority. As soon as the humans finished their meal, he would escort them out of the compound and into the slaughtering house where they would spend the day butchering the giant tondars. Already he could hear the docile beasts braying their morning greeting, unaware that it would be their last. Several hundred of the tondars and a smaller amount of the striped arixiaths—cousins of those used to pull the transport barges—would be slaughtered in ten of the outside compounds to provide the daily food supply for Buzthara.

Leading the lumbering humans along the well-worn path that led to the slaughter house, Arnth heard the crashing sound of a large body of running men. A score of humans, half-dressed in animal skins, rushed the work party with spears and crudely fashioned short swords. As he lashed out at the attacking men with his sting whip, he wondered where the humans had found so much metal. Armed with only the whip and a dagger, he soon found himself sorely pressed by three of the shouting humans. Raids such as this were infrequent and there were only three of the huge Boidae guardsmen protecting the work party; then only two, as one of the giants fell with a spear embedded in his throat.

Arnth screamed in pain as a heavy sword blow took off his whip hand at the wrist. A bright red fountain arched toward the sky and he began to slowly sink down. The last thing he saw was a group of strange humans push through the attackers and circle his bleeding body. As black night fell, he heard their foreign babble fade away into silence, and then the beating of wings as Cthor's minions came to carry him away.

"I know you'd like to be a sociologist, Thorstein," answered his teacher, "but why don't you try for a more realistic goal?"

"Yeah, what would they want with a bastard like you," whispered a voice from behind. "After all, your father could be a mute or sport, and you'd never know."

"Shut up," he screamed, as his voice echoed louder and louder through the valleys of his mind.

Those of you who pass the tests and prove to be sound in body and mind," droned the Elder, "will be allowed a name and membership in the Elapidae Clan. Those of you who fail will be dealt with mercifully and sent on your way to Cthor's realm with honor."

"Now, I must warn you all," continued the Instructor, "that if you fail this sociology Eligibility Exam, there will be no more chances. There are, as you are all well aware, far more applicants than available positions. . . ."

Arnth felt the smooth/warmth of Sandri as he rubbed his neck and shoulders against hers in the beginning gambit of the mating ritual. He felt her press back with obvious enthusiasm and couldn't help but wonder if she would be reacting the same if it were his blood that stained the sand of the Pit rather than his opponent's.

Pushing aside the razor-sharp leaves with his hands, Veblen forced his body to keep moving through the orange and vermillion jungle. His mind was burning with fever while his body was bleeding from a thousand hairline cuts. Camp. He had to reach the camp and use his med-kit. Because if he stopped moving or trying, his bones would become just one more decoration on this death world.

As the knife sliced into the human's chest cavity, Arnth took another deep drink from the golden chalice.

"Think you're better than the rest of us," cried the childish voice from above. He tried to move, but his arms and shoulders were pinned to the ground by the larger boy's knees. Veblen felt his head slam into the hard pavement again and again.

"But I thought my initiation was over," protested Arnth. *"I know the secret signs, the shibboleths, the*

sacred litany, and I have tasted the life fluid of the enemy."

"To be a Mamba," hissed the wizened priest, *"one must partake in all of the sacraments. You must kill one of the human beasts with your own hands and bring back his still-warm heart and place it on the altar.*

"This is your first case, Veblen," stated the Director of Extraterrestrial Investigations, "and I can't emphasize enough its importance in terms of your career. There are a lot of people, big people, Veblen, who would like to see you fail. Don't."

"It's my blood pouring to the ground! Why doesn't it hurt? Great Serpent, don't leave me. I don't want to die."

"Thor!" cried a voice, from the edge of the abyss. "Are you all right?"

Veblen opened his eyes and then closed them rapidly to block out the stabbing light. His mind was a whirlpool of spinning thoughts and images which were moving faster and faster, until at the center they became a blur of white light. Like the rising sun, it grew in brilliance and intensity, casting its rays over the hills and canyons of his mind. When it reached its midday apex he suddenly realized who he was and what had happened.

"Can you hear me?" asked the voice, which he identified as Vera's.

"Yes," he answered, opening his eyes very slowly. "Everything is coming back."

"What happened? You've been comatose for over forty-eight hours."

"Forty-eight hours!" he shouted, and then winced as a flash of pain penetrated his head like a cutting laser. "They made a mistake during the Intercortical RNA Memory Transfer. Instead of giving me the RNA from a human mind, they transferred it from an Ophidian brain. A sick and twisted mind," he added, with sudden fervor. "One that hated human beings with an animal passion."

"But how could that have happened?"

"I don't know," he answered coldly. "But I intend to find out!"

"You don't think it was done on purpose. Do you?"

"I can't think of any other reasonable explanation."

"But who?"

"There are at least half a dozen possibilities, including that twittering friend of yours."

"What right do you have to talk like that about someone you don't even really know. Just because he's a little different. . . ."

"Different!" exclaimed Veblen, in mock horror. "He's a one-man freak show."

"You're impossible."

"At least I'm not an imposer or impostor."

"You don't need a memory transfer," said Vera disdainfully, "you need a heart transplant."

Before he could form a reply she spun around and walked out of the med-room.

"Ahhh," he cried at the blank walls with impotent fury. Not only had Vera gotten in the last word, but he was stuck here in the med-room with a skull-shattering ache.

"Is everything all right in here," asked a middle-aged woman, dressed in a plain white tunic.

"I think so, Doctor," moaned Veblen.

"I'm glad to see that you've recovered consciousness," said the doctor. "I have never seen an experienced Investigator have such an adverse reaction to an Intercortical Memory Transfer."

"Well, normally we don't," answered Veblen stiffly, "when we're given the correct transfer."

"I'm not sure I understand what you're talking about, Investigator."

"Apparently, someone injected the RNA from an Ophidian brain into my cranium, instead of the human RNA I was supposed to receive."

The doctor took a deep breath and then sat down at her desk and punched several keys on the Medical Registry. She looked at the flat grey screen for almost a minute, and then turned towards her patient. "According to my records, you were given the RNA residue of a sixty-two-year-old human male. Before recovery, he was suffering from a coronary thrombosis and the med-unit was able to transport him to the life-support systems about fifteen minutes before termination. It also says that the chromosomal compatibility index was high enough that he was considered to be the optimum donor."

"Were there any Ophidians brought aboard the Collecting Craft?"

"One or two, for further study," said the doctor as she once again began to peck at the Medical Registry keys. "Here we are. The first subject: male, approximately fifty years of age, right hand amputated at wrist. . . ."

"And his name is Arnth and he was a member of the Elapidae Clan."

"But how do you know?"

"I have his persona in my head."

"But that is impossible, Investigator," objected the doctor. "Each subject is properly identified and labelled. Someone would have had to deliberately tamper with the RNA maintenance receptacles, and that is out of the question."

"Who else has access to this room?"

"Just the Captain, myself, Dr. Harvington, and the maintenance mate. You don't think it was done deliberately?"

"I am on an important mission, and there may be a person or persons aboard who would rather not see me complete it successfully."

"Well, I can assure you, Investigator," said the doctor formally, "that the RNA injections were done according to strict procedure—and there were *no* complications."

"I'm quite sure that everything was done as normal, but how long was the RNA stored before I underwent the memory transfer?"

"Several days . . . I see what you mean."

"Plenty of time for someone to have made a substitution and even reprogram the Medical Registry."

"An ingenuous method of eliminating an opponent," said the doctor, thinking out loud, "without ever technically committing murder. It should have succeeded. and probably would have with anyone who didn't have your self-assurance and strong ego."

"I'd better get up and see what I can find."

"Hold it right there," said the doctor in her most professional tone of voice. "You've been delirious for over forty-eight standard hours, and your body is going to need time to recuperate and build its strength. Now we can speed up that process considerably, but you're still going to have to stay in this med-room until you've recovered."

Veblen could tell by her set expression that he was going to have to concede. "If I'm going to be stuck here, could you, at least, have a scanner brought in so I can do a little research. That way I won't feel that I am completely wasting my time."

Oblivious to his little barb, the doctor answered, "I think that can be arranged. I'll have Vera bring in several of your cassettes. I'm sure she won't mind."

Veblen winced.

"By the way, where is she? Every minute that you were unconscious she was right by your side. I wonder why she would leave the moment you pull out of your delirium?"

Veblen contracted into a fetal ball, wishing that there was some place he could hide in the clear homeostatic life-support environment that surrounded him like a plastic womb. Every time he thought he understood that woman, she had to turn on him. Why hadn't she said anything? Or did she enjoy watching him make an ass out of himself? And all this time he had thought there was something going on between her and the Dauphin. Holy Sanity, was his head beginning to hurt!

Six

AFTER THE LAST MAGI had taken his seat at the table in the Regent's Room, Magus Avanar rose to his feet and stated calmly: "The Great Plan is in greater danger today than it has been since the founding of the university, twenty-four thousand years ago."

The Master Magus had a reputation for understatement, and his audience's reaction was the same as it would have been had the massive stone walls around them suddenly, and without reason, toppled down upon them. Time and sound seemed to recede, until a sudden wave of clamoring voices broke through the room.

When order had been restored, Magus Rohne, an Elder of the Elapidae Clan and distinguished scholar, asked for permission to speak. "Master Magus, I am afraid that I do not understand your pronouncement. For as each year has passed, I have seen the university gain more stature and prestige. In following the dictates of the Grand Plan, we have made significant steps towards joining together the talents and abilities of both the humans and the Ophidians; thereby, proving, not only that the two species can work together, but that they are complementary. It has been this amalgamation, within the last ten years, which has provided the soil for the new technology we see growing around us. Hand in hand, human and Ophidian have made a great leap towards a new common culture and a roadway to the stars."

"There is no doubt that we have made some impressive achievements," said the Master Magus, his eyes coming to rest on the three humans seated at the table, dressed in the saffron robes of the Brethren. "It is also true that most of these advancements have been made within the cloistered halls of the university, and not in the back alleys of Buzthara. We have had very little success in changing the attitudes and prejudices of the average clansman within the capital and throughout the provinces. The majority of them believe in the same half-truths and superstitions as their ancestors did during the time of the Oligarchy. Fellow Magi, we have failed to take our message to the streets and win the hearts of our fellow clansmen, and in our arrogance we have jeopardized the success of the Great Plan."

"Things are not as black as you have painted," cried one of the younger Brethren, who had just recently passed the rites of office.

"You don't think so," asked the Master Magus rhetorically, "then answer me this. Would you risk walking the back alleyways of Buzthara late at night, dressed in your robes of office?"

The young Magi paused momentarily and then waved his left hand back and forth in negation.

"Well, I wouldn't either," said Magus Avanar, "though, when I was your age I would have done so

54

without hesitation. Is this not true?"

Almost all of the older members agreed in unison.

"Therefore, one must conclude," continued the Master, "that our position within the community has deteriorated within the past twenty-five years. But why?"

"Is it possible," asked Magus Rohne, "that the majority of our people feel threatened by our achievements, and are afraid they may find themselves supplanted by the humans, who are their superiors in the creation and repair of mechanical objects?"

"Quite possible," answered Magus Avanar. I'm sure that many see our industrialization as a threat to a millenniums' old way of life. Take, for example, a member of the Natrix Tribe, a bargeman, who has spent all of his life guiding the large transport barges from one city to another through the underground system of canals and river ways. How will this tribesman feel when he sees one of the new paddle-wheel barges moving through the canals—free of its Arixiath team, and crewed by two or three bargemen instead of the customary five or six? Imagine his anger and chagrin when he finds out that one of these men is the craft's human mechanic."

"I can understand his resentment," said one of the humans. "But, as of yet, we have fewer than twenty of the new paddle barges in operation."

"True, but the bargemen are smart enough to realize that as soon as they prove their worth, they will quickly replace the older and less efficient barges. Which means that he, an Ophidian, will be replaced by a human-designed and manufactured craft. That is alien to his whole way of life."

"Then it is up to us to prove to him that we are improving his way of life," said the human, "for we are giving him the time to do something better with his life than pushing and guiding a canal barge."

"I agree. But unfortunately we have spent far more of our time designing and developing machinery, than in preparing our people, human and Ophidian, for the coming industrial revolution."

"True," stated Magus Rohne, "but I do not see how this threatens the very existence of the Great Plan?"

"The recent reappearance of the secret societies— the Mambas, the Cobra Cult, the Bushmasters, and Asp Assassins—along with the intensifying human prejudice, have created a climate favorable to the growth of the reactionary elements of our society. Some are even conducting secret deals and alliances with off-worlders in an attempt to usurp the legitimate power of the Council and the Clan Elders, and return to the tyranny of the old Oligarchy."

"But that is impossible!"

"They'll never get away with it," shouted another.

When quiet had again been restored, Magus Soth, the oldest and most venerated of the Magi, slowly stood up. His multicolored bands of red, white, and black had faded with age to an almost even grey, and his forked tongue seemed to stumble over his crooked teeth as it tested the air. When it seemed as though the very air itself would crackle with tension, he began to speak. "Master Magus and distinguished colleagues. Having approached that time of life where one can feel the misty breath of death, I find myself most distressed by what I have just heard. In just a matter of minutes, I have been made to feel that all I have worked and fought for is but a sham. I hope that the Master can substantiate his claims; for if he cannot, I will personally ask for his resignation from his high office."

There was a murmur of accord.

Magus Avanar looked at the old Magus with compassion and then began to speak, "Magus Soth, I can both appreciate and understand your distress and I share your concern. For it has only been recently that I have become aware of the changes going on around us. It was only several weeks ago that I received word that the off-worlders had established a camp just north of Zendo, and that they were seen there digging in the ground with their machines. Soon thereafter, I questioned the First Elder about their activity and he admitted that they were working with his permission—a flagrant violation of the Council's rights—and then he stated that the off-worlders have promised to provide us interstellar spacecraft and advanced weaponry so that we may reestablish our power in this sector of the universe."

"But that is not *his* decision to make," cried the ancient Ophidian.

"I know, and I told him that I would call a special meeting of the Elder Council to closely examine his actions—although I'm no longer sure that I can obtain enough votes to pass a motion of censure. There are many who secretly sympathize with the restoration of the Oligarchy."

"But this is madness," cried one of the Magi. "Such a path will only lead our people to doom."

"It will be the end of everything the university has worked for!"

"Folly!"

"I explained this to him," continued the Master Magus, "but his lust for power and spoils has taken him beyond the land of reason. It is up to us to find a way to stop him, for I am almost sure the Council will bend before his will—leading to disaster."

"But how?"

"First, we must learn the true extent of his power and influence among the Clans and Tribes."

"I'm sure that we can win the support of Mar Verdon and the Bitis Tribe," said Magus Rohne. Next spring marks their assent to power."

"We will send emissaries to the Viper and Atheris Tribes as well," said Magus Avanar, "and see if we can enlist their support also. I only hope that we have enough time."

"How much longer before we reach earthside," asked Vera, her voice betraying just a hint of nervousness.

"We should reach Seker's stratosphere within a few minutes," answered Veblen patronizingly; after all, he had gone through these procedures many times before. "Then I'll put the controls on manual override and set us down ten or fifteen klicks away from Buzthara."

"Do you think we'll have any difficulty gaining entrance into the city?"

"I don't think so, Vera. This merchant disguise gives us a lot of room for improvisation, since it's not at all unusual for one to travel to the surface and even trade with the Thadrons. With the recent increase in industrialization upon Seker, there has been a tremendous increase in surface operations— including some trading with the bands of humans, or Thadrons, who inhabit large portions of the globe."

"Lack of information," said Vera, with distaste, "is just one of the difficulties of having a female persona in a patriarchal society. The only things my persona is familiar with are greeting and serving rituals. I wouldn't even no how to cook a meal without the servants' help."

"If I would have known that was going to bother you, I would have seen to it that you were given the persona of a lower-caste human." Seeing that Vera was not taking his suggestion with the same humor that prompted it, he quickly added, "I'll do my best to give you a comprehensive briefing."

"Thanks," she said, with acidic sarcasm.

He began laughing and a moment later she joined in. As they were momentarily joined in humor, he couldn't help but wonder if it was their similarities, rather than their differences, that kept them at each other's throats. For he was honest enough to admit that others had accused him of many of the same traits that he found so objectionable in her; such as her insensitivity, lack of warmth, rigidity, intolerance, and underdeveloped sense of humor. Though, on the other hand, she had many of the traits he admired; such as her efficiency, diligence, intelligence, integrity, and strong sense of duty.

"Go ahead," she joked. "Drop upon my head the manna of your wisdom, so that I may taste the bread of knowledge."

"Your wish is my command. The basic unit of Ophidian society, unlike most human societies where the young are born live, is the clan and its subdivision, the tribe. On Seker, there are five major clans: the Colubrinae, the Elapidae, the Viperidae, the Boidae, and the Hydrophidae. Each of these has several tribal units. Each clan maintains its own nurseries, or crèches, where the young are raised and taught the basic fundamentals of Ophidian society. The average Ophidian matures several years before his human counterpart, and undertakes his rite of passage at about age ten or eleven. By maintaining a strict control over the number of eggs within the hatchery, and by requiring vigorous mental and physical standards for passage into the clan, the Ophidians have managed to increase their general well-being and keep their population growth in check."

"But what happens to those who don't meet their high mental and physical standards?"

"They are painlessly and humanely put to death."

"That doesn't sound too humane to me."

"I agree that it isn't one of the more pleasant means of population control, but the Ophidians view it as a better alternative than overcrowding, mass-psychosis, and starvation. Now, once the child has become an adult, he is admitted into the clan and assigned to a tribe on the basis of his ancestral background and tribal markings. The tribe, in effect, becomes the new adult's extended family, political representative, and occupational guide. The new adult, however, is given no choice about his admittance into the tride. But the tribe will grant him, for life, not only his way of life but social status too, for the Ophidians are racially segregated by clan and tribe. The Ophidian races or tribal units are separated by traits that, in the long view, are more decorative than functional differences. To a greater or lesser degree, they all share the same physical and mental attributes; they have two ears, two elliptical eyes, a forked tongue, two facial heat sensors, two arms, two legs, and lay eggs. Where they differ, like humanity, is in ornamentation; skin coloration, banding, and design. The clans themselves vary greatly in size, function, and status. While the Colubrinae Clan has the most members, its clansmen do most of the menial work, and have the least status of any of the clans."

"Where do the humans fit in their society?"

"That's difficult to explain, Vera. I've never run across anything comparable. But, if you were to look at each clan as being a separate caste—a dubious comparison, at best, since several of the clans have horizontal status, rather than vertical status—you would have to consider the human caste as being the lowest; that is, the pariah or untouchable. However, this doesn't mean that there aren't humans who are wealthy and in important positions within society. Generally, the humans occupy those positions which the Ophidians find repugnant because of disinclination, inability, and tradition. In fact, now that Ophidian society is beginning to experience the birth throes of industrialization, the human beings are gaining, as a class, more importance and status. A change which might well be responsible for the rapid increase in human persecution and intolerance—of which, I could tell you a great deal."

"Fascinating," exclaimed Vera, her eyes glowing above the veil she wore as part of her disguise. "You should record your findings when we return to Anomia. No one has ever seen this society with such clarity!"

"But then, no one has had to go through my learning experience, either," said Veblen with a grimace. "I'd be happy to never go through another experience like that again."

"Do you still think that someone deliberately switched personas on you?"

"Someone had to have," said Veblen thoughtfully, "but I don't know who or why. Although, I will admit that it will turn out to be an advantage when we reach Seker. I'm just hoping that when we land we don't find a reception committee waiting for us."

"So that's why you told me to bring a laser along?"

"Could be," said Veblen, who was turning in response to a warning buzz from the control panel. Veblen sat down on the contour seat and began to scan the operations panel. Forty-eight kilometers was the digital heighth readout. He switched off the autopilot and pressed the button for manual operation. Whenever possible, Veblen preferred to land the shuttle himself, convinced the human element allowed for a more surreptitious landing. Suddenly, the shuttle craft refused to respond to manual controls!

Veblen tried to reduce power, but nothing happened. The craft's controls were locked into place. He flicked on the emergency override system and ordered: "Condition Red. Condition Red. Place all equipment on manual control. This is an emergency order."

"What's wrong?" cried Vera.

Veblen motioned her to silence and then listened carefully to the ship's answer. "Emergency request is unauthorized. Emergency request is unauthorized. Craft will continue on present course. Priority Ten. Priority Ten. Priority Ten. . . ."

"What is going on!" shouted Vera, trying to make herself heard over the mad drone of the ship's computer.

"I'm not sure," answered Veblen, not wanting to voice his fears. What *was* wrong with the shuttle craft? Had someone tampered with the ship's computer? A chill began to work its way up his spine. Their speed was now over Mach III. They were on a collision course! Thirty-four kilometers. Not much time!

"Cut the power cable," he yelled to Vera. She looked at him questioningly. "Use your laser," he ordered.

He sighed with relief as she tore out of the cabin.

He watched himself cross his fingers, and thought angrily. Where did *that* come from? He felt the craft jump as the power cut out. A tiny flame of hope sputtered and then grew as the retro-rockets responded to their controls. Twenty-eight kilometers!

Vera came running out of the engine room and through the cabin to her seat. He heard the sound of labored breathing as she fastened herself down. Then he felt her fingers working on his safety webbing and he gave her a smile.

Four of the eight retros were now in position. Would he have time to turn the rest? Eighteen kilometers.

"Can you stop it?" asked Vera, her voice a high soprano.

"No," he answered. "But maybe I can slow it down enough to give us a chance."

Only two more retros to go. Twelve kilometers!

"Priority Ten. Priority Ten. Priority Ten . . ." continued the computer in its atonal voice.

Why wouldn't the retro move faster? Was it because of the power disruption, or was it that time was slowing under the focus of his intense concentration? One retro to go. Fifteen kilometers! Maybe it was him. A shrill scream from the ship's hull began to drown out the droning computer.

Nine kilometers.

Speed still increasing! Last retro slowly moving into place. Unbearable heat.

Seven kilometers.

Retro still moving.

Five kilometers!

Final retro synchronized. Piercing scream from the outside.

Three kilometers to the planet's surface.

Pain! Ship vibrating and shaking. One. . . .

"Fire!"

A thunder clap. The ship rocking and screeching as though it had been smashed by a giant fist. Debris flying through the cabin. Another scream. Was it his voice or Vera's. Insides feeling as though they were being pushed into the back of the seat. Control panel no longer functioning.

A bone-shattering crash. A sea of pain. Black oblivion. . . .

Seven

THE DISTANT RINGING broke like waves against the shoals of the First Elder's mind, radiating ripples that disturbed the still water of his attention. Raising his head from the meditation stance, he opened the floodgates of consciousness. Ever since the upsetting meeting with the Master Magus, the First Elder had increased his meditation time in an effort to purge the bile of emotion from his system. He was convinced that his prolonged contacts with the off-worlders was to blame for his shameful loss of emotional control; after all, humans radiated a miasma of conflicting emotions which permeated the air and infected everyone within reach.

The bell began to chime again and the First Elder nodded to his personal attendant, a massive Pythoninae with emerald skin, who walked over to the ornately-carved door and opened a small panel. The Pythoninae stood in statuesque silence as the person outside chanted the words of invitation and then, when the ritual had come to an end, unbolted the latch and slipped into the shadows at the far end of the room.

Through the doorway walked Counsellor Donal and an off-worlder wearing the purple robes of his order.

When he and the counsellor had finished the abbreviated greeting ritual—used when in the presence of one-not-of-the-true-race—the First Elder examined the off-worlder satisfying himself that it was the same human he had talked to before. Like a pale white worm, the human stood blinking in the room's dim light. The humans were almost blind in the twilight world of the Ophidian subterranean cities, and the First Elder looked upon this as further proof of their basic inferiority. After a quick study—he prided himself on his ability to distinguish one human from another—he decided that this was indeed the off-worlder who called himself Brother Bernard.

The First Elder held out his ring hand for the Brother's attentions. The Brother bowed, grasped his ring hand, kissed the Elder's ring of office, and then walked back four paces and came to a stop. The First Elder forced himself to hide the shudder that threatened to shake his body—would he ever get used to that horrid custom—and nodded graciously to the Brother, thereby granting him permission to speak.

"I have answered your call as quickly as possible," stated Brother Bernard, "and pray that you and yours are well."

"The Sacred Egg lies uncracked and the Clan flourishes. I pray that yours does as well."

"We are doing well, Elder."

The First Elder sensed an undercurrent of impatience within the Brother and was tempted to prolong his greeting, but decided against it. At this time, there was little to be gained in upsetting the human.

"Your messenger was adamant about me meeting

you right away," continued the Brother. "Is anything wrong?"

"Yes. The political situation in Buzthara has changed significantly since our last meeting. Several important groups have become opposed to having off-worlders use Seker as an illegal base of operations within the Magellanic Clouds."

"But Elder . . . we obtained your permission. Isn't that enough?"

"Ordinarily, yes," answered the First Elder. "But my decisions can be overruled by the Elder Council."

"Is this probable," asked the Brother, his body radiating an odor of fear and anxiety.

This was the strongest reaction the Elder had ever gotten from the Brother, and he began to wonder what the off-worlders were really after. For a second he contemplated disengaging his support and ordering them to leave. But would they go? Then, where would that leave him? He needed their help if he was to turn his dream into reality. It wasn't right, that the greatest race in the galaxy should be held prisoner on an insignificant ball of mud. It would be better to die than to continue such a meaningless existence. What concessions could he wrest from the human? He must be careful or otherwise the Brother might discover his intentions.

"Yes, it is probable," he lied. He knew that he was safe in it, no human could ever hope to understand the complex system of personal relationships and interclan alliances that made up Ophidian politics. "The Master Magus has promised to contest my decision before a special meeting of the Council and to press for my dismissal for abuse of power."

"Who is the Master Magus?"

"He is an Ophidian of limited power, but great influence. As Master Magus, he is head of the Micrurus Tribe and spokesman for the University of Jarazia and the Magi. The Magi is a sacred organization of scholars and alchemists who plot the course of the race. They are revered by the populace and held in high esteem by the clans. An attack on one of their person is held to be a grave violation of the law. Obviously, their sentiments carry a great deal of weight among the masses and the Clan Elders."

"I see," said the Brother nervously. "Isn't there anything you can do?"

The trap has been set, thought the Elder. "The Council must be shown some tangible evidence of your commitment to our cause."

"I wouldn't call three interplanetary spacecraft *in*-tangible," returned the Brother.

The Elder silenced him with a glare and then continued. "Many of them already see this gift as but an opening gambit by your organization to win our support for your own ends." The Elder was almost positive he saw a startled look flash across Brother Bernard's face. Who was using whom? He would have to keep a careful eye on the off-worlders. "Therefore," he resumed, "some further demonstration of your sincerity might go a long way in disproving these charges."

What does he want now, Brother Bernard asked himself, as he tried to evade the snake-man's piercing gaze. He was just not the right man to be negotiating with these over-evolved reptiles. There was something cold and remote about them that made him feel uneasy and vulnerable. He wasn't sure whether it was their hooded glare, their expressionless faces, or their sinuous movements that bothered him most. Even their lack of emotion was unnerving; it seemed sinister and calculated, rather than logical and lofty like that of the Proctors' or the Prime Monitor.

Before this assignment, he had judged himself uninvolved with his animal nature, and almost clear of all human emotion. Yet now he found himself weathering emotional tempests, the like of which he hadn't felt since adolescence. If only he had been able to refuse this assignment when he had first watched the Solidos of Seker, and felt himself break out in a cold sweat. But he knew why he had not done so. His refusal would have meant a review of status by the Prime Monitor, and his submission to emotion would have been duly noted. Then he might have found himself reclassified and he might have had to start all over again as an Alpha; or he might have even been purged from the Brotherhood. He had to learn to control his human weaknesses or he would never become a Clear, and as such, eligible for the implants that would make him more than human.

"We need further proof of your intentions," repeated the Elder, through thin lips.

His unblinking eyes seeming to peer through the veil of flesh that covered the Brother's soul, and he tried to dismiss the gooseflesh that ran up and down his arms. "Haven't we promised to provide you with star ships of your own, as soon as we can slip them through the Anomian net," said the Brother.

"This is true," answered the Elder, "but does tomorrow's feast still today's hunger pangs?"

"But what could we provide that would make any difference," demanded the Brother, his voice breaking.

The First Elder appeared to coil back on his throne and then his head darted forward, as though he were going to strike. "A large shipment of weapons would be sufficient."

"Weapons!" He wondered what they were intended for. The Proctor would not be pleased about this at all. This was supposed to have been a simple operation. And it would have been one, if they hadn't had a run-in with a fleet of Anomian cruisers and lost their escorts, plus suffered heavy damage to the reaction drive of *The Sword of Wrath*. And now the whole expedition was threatened by the Elder's unexpected avarice. "I don't know if that will be possible," said the Brother, his voice edged with sarcasm. "After all, we're not on a trading mission."

"I must have a firm commitment before the Council meeting," stated the Elder. "Otherwise, I can guarantee nothing. Remember, it is my political life that is at stake."

"As well as the future of your people," added Brother Bernard. Plus much, much more, he thought to himself. "I will talk to my superior, Elder, and let you know his decision. He won't be pleased. He was under the erroneous impression that you ran things around here."

Seeing an angry glow behind the Elder's eyes, Brother Bernard felt a surge of satisfaction; and this time the emotion didn't bother him one little bit.

"It seemed very obvious to me," said Veblen, as he limped along the overgrown path, "that someone doesn't want our mission to be successful."

"So you don't think the crash was an accident, then," said Vera, her gown all rumpled and creased. Even with the veil, it was quite obvious that her face was bruised and cut and one eye was circled by a dark purple ring.

"That crash was no more an accident, than the memory transfer substitution," said Veblen. He looked even worse than Vera. The wreck of the shuttle craft had left him pinned to the control panel. Only a determined effort on Vera's part had freed him from the wreckage before the craft had burst into flame. As it was, his body was covered with scratches and bruises, and his shirt was missing one sleeve. "That attempt," he continued, "was more covert, since it was aboard the ship where my death would have lead to an investigation. But now the *Daybreak* is several million kilometers away and out of the range of our portable high-frequency transmitters."

"But who is behind all of this?"

"Undoubtably the same group that is supplying the Ophidians with interplanetary spacecraft," answered Veblen, sitting down on a fallen log which stretched across the trail. At one time, the surrounding area had been heavily forested; but now the landscape was studded with velvet stumps crowded by tangled underbrush. After massaging his injured leg for a while, he continued: "By wrecking the shuttle, our assailants have placed our mission in jeopardy, though I'm sure they didn't plan on us leaving the craft alive."

"Thanks to you that didn't happen. . . ."

"Don't praise me," interrupted Veblen. "I only did what I had to do and nothing else. Anyway, they have destroyed most of our equipment and have made it impossible to contact the *Daybreak* until we reach Buzthara—by which time it will probably be too late to reach the ship before she makes the Stromborg Shift."

"Maybe if we hurried, we could reach our Informant in time to make contact and have some of our equipment replaced with undamaged equipment?"

"It's possible," said Veblen, "but I really don't think there will be that much need for most of what we brought with us."

"But what are we going to do without most of our weapons and the ship's computer to correlate our findings?"

Veblen took a deep breath and then exhaled slowly. "We're going to do it the way it is usually done, with hard work, sweat, and intuition. When you're in the field, you don't have time to run to the ship and re-check your data and let the computer mull over your facts; not that it would do any good anyway. That's one of the problems with the human race today; no one is willing to make a statement without first consulting a computer on the probability of its validity. Almost nobody is willing to take a chance on being wrong unless there's a computer he can blame."

"Then what do you suggest," asked Vera disspiritedly, her body slumped with fatigue. "I don't even know how we're going to make it to the city's main gate before nightfall, and I certainly don't want to spend the night out here in the open."

"We're not headed towards the main gate," said Veblen in puzzlement until he suddenly realized that he hadn't told Vera his plans. He noted, for the first time, that one of his major difficulties in working with other people was his unconscious assumption that once he had made a logical and necessary decision, that it was obvious to everyone around him. "Since my persona spent some time in this area, I have a lot of information on some of the alternate access routes into the city. Using this information, I came to the conclusion that it would be much shorter to travel to one of the air ducts, which are within eight or nine kilometers, rather than travel to the main gate, which is over forty kilometers from where we crashed."

"Air ducts?"

"They're giant chimneys that come up from the subterranean caverns and tunnels, providing fresh air for the Ophidian's underground world. Besides helping to circulate the air, they are equipped with hand-holds for travel."

"But I thought we were supposed to meet our Informant outside of the main gate?"

"We were, but there is no way we would have made it today. Anyway, there's an alternate meeting place inside Buzthara, at the Temple Plaza, where he'll be waiting at noon every day for the next three days."

As Veblen rose to his feet, Vera asked, "How much farther do we have to travel?"

"Less than half a kilometer," he answered, gingerly placing his weight on his right leg. "You can tell we're getting nearer to the city because of the age of these tree stumps. According to my persona's memory, the price of firewood has been rising over the years as the loggers have had to go farther afield. Well, come on. Let's go," he ordered, as Vera continued to sit wearily on the log.

At last, she offered her hand. Women, thought Veblen, as he gave her his hand and helped her up. However, he didn't notice, as they began to walk down the rough trail, that he forgot to let go.

Eight

BROTHER BERNARD PRESSED the Heraldkey nervously and waited for the cabin door to slide open. As he walked into the Proctor's cabin, he did his best to block the turmoil he felt churning inside. Using the techniques and disciplines learned as a student, he blanked his mind of all thoughts and images and took partial control of his autonomic nervous system. Then, at last, the cool waters of serenity began to seep through his mind submerging his fears and anxieties. Although one thought, thrusting out of his sea of contentment like the tip of an iceberg, continued to haunt him—how long would it be before once again he would be forced to come face to face with one of those barely human reptiles—this thought too slipped beneath the calm waters and he stood before his superior calm and composed.

The Proctor, in spite of being the ultimate in the man/machine synthesis, displayed none of the discordant mechanical attributes that made the nearby cyborg Guardian—four meters of flesh and metal—so gruesome. It was only the Proctor's unusual height and inhuman eyes, capable of spanning the whole light spectrum, that revealed his mechanized soul. Eyes the color of stainless steel which coldly measured, judged, and filed away all that passed beneath their gaze. He stood two and a half meters tall, with a physique so perfectly proportioned that it bespoke of origins other than the womb. A black tunic, with a silver crescent inside a circle of red emblazoned over the heart, covered his torso while black tights concealed his lower limbs. His well-chiselled face was marred by the ascetic chill which had frozen his features into a pose of studied disinterest. Brother Bernard, accustomed to religious analogies, was never able to decide if the Proctor's face resembled that of a hard god or a just devil.

"You are upset," stated the Proctor. "I take it, that all is not well."

Brother Bernard started. His control cracked like a pane of glass. The Proctor had read him like a simple layman peering right through his facade of tranquility. If he was so transparent, how would he ever become a Clear and eligible for Conversion. Waves of doubt and fear began to break within his mind, and he felt as though he were once again a young Alpha—battered and tossed by storms of feeling and emotion, unaware of the exercises that could still their fury.

"Brother," called the Proctor. "Remember what is recorded in the Unor. 'Hold your ears tightly against the sirens of emotion, before they send you crashing into the shoals of irrationality.' For it is not a sin for the unclean to feel, it is the curse of all flesh. The sin is in not fighting the siren's song."

The Proctor's unexpected support, instead of the rebuke he knew he justly deserved, enabled Brother

Bernard to strengthen his resolve and still the temptest raging inside his head.

After allowing the Brother time to pull himself together, the Proctor asked, "Now, what did the Ophidian leader demand of us this time?"

Brother Bernard swallowed. "The Ophidian Elder wants further aid for his continued support." Just for an instant, the Brother could have sworn that he saw a spark of anger shine in the Proctor's silver eyes, but such an occurrence was inconceivable and he promptly dismissed it as simply being a play of light.

"If the Anomian fleet hadn't destroyed our sister ships and damaged *The Sword of Wrath,* we would have completed this mission and been done with this extortion long ago."

"How much longer will it be before the recovery crew has obtained enough fuel to replace that which was lost?" asked Brother Bernard. He had spent much of the last two weeks on Seker in the underground city of Buzthara, and he was hoping there had been a change of schedule for the better.

"According to the Chief Engineer, it will be at least another week. The only fissionable fuel they have been able to find is a low grade uranium ore, which takes a long time to refine. Once we have sufficient fuel for our journey, we will complete our mission and wait up here with impunity until *The Sword of Wrath* is ready to depart."

"But Proctor, why don't we finish our mission now and forget about the fuel for the reaction drive. After all, we're over two thousand kilometers from Seker, and I've heard of other ships which have successfully made a shift into hyperspace this close to a planetary body."

"If there were no sun nearby, I might take the

chance," answered the Proctor. "But, as far as I know, there has never been a successful Stromborg Shift made within the gravitational pull of a large star. At best, the ship would be caught in a whirlpool of solar gravity which would tear it into subatomic particles. We would find ourself at the mercy of titanic forces magnified and distorted in that elsewhere dimension of hyperspace. This mission is too important to be sabotaged by our impatience, though I think that this may be just the right time to start Operation Psi."

"Good," said Brother Bernard, pleased to have something concrete to work on. "I'll contact all my operatives so soon as I return to Buzthara. Do you think we should go ahead with the abduction before our mining operations are concluded on the surface?" he added, as an afterthought.

"It will be some time before they connect us with abduction, and the mining and refining operations are far from any populated center. We will be gone before they are in any position to hamper our efforts there."

"You know best, Proctor," said Brother Bernard, "but I have a feeling that the Ophidians may be more dangerous than we have estimated."

"I'm afraid, Brother Bernard, that the mantle of flesh lies much heavier on you than most of your brethren."

Brother Bernard felt his blood turn to ice water, and it took all of his willpower to keep his body from betraying his inner tension.

The Proctor studied him for several seconds, as though examining an interesting specimen. "While most in my place would see it as their obligation to have you defrocked for your lack of self-control, I only see a greater need, on your part, to shed your cloak of flesh and find true peace in the man/machine synthesis."

Is it possible he pities me, Brother Bernard asked himself, or is this just a ploy to help maintain my stability until he no longer has any need of my services?

"Now," said the Proctor, "what demands do these Ophidians make upon us?"

"The First Elder claims that his people need further proof of our sincerity. He wants us to supply him with a shipment of arms and ammunition."

"I don't like these sudden demands. What are the alternatives if we don't comply."

"He told me that there was a possibility that he might be removed from office, and that would not suit our purposes. If they ordered us to leave, it would endanger Operation Psi and place our mining. . . ."

"It is not necessary to draw me a picture," stated the Proctor, his monotone voice rising almost imperceptibly in volume. "I am well aware of the negative sequence of events which, in all probability, would occur should an opposition party rise to power. Therefore, we shall meet his demands; although I expect you to convince him that there shall be no more of this extortion in the future."

"There will be no more."

"Good. Now, I think that two or three hundred primitive projectile weapons, along with two or three hundred thousand rounds of ammunition, should be more than enough to satisfy the Elder."

"Certainly," said the Brother. "I'm sure he will find them a vast improvement over the crossbows and dartguns now in use."

"I think so. I'll have to bring up part of the recovery crew from the surface and have them go to work on the weapons in the machine shop. Of course, this will mean a further delay of our mining and refining operations. I hope our Ophidian ally enjoys his Pyrrhic victory, for he will pay a heavy price when his people learn of their loss.

Veblen braced his body, set his everlux on a rocky ledge, and told Vera to jump. The impact of her body falling against his almost sent him sprawling, but he managed to maintain his balance. Vera was all over him, like an Edefin sucker fish, and he silently cursed the jagged pain in his leg that made him unable to enjoy what would have otherwise been a pleasurable experience.

"You can let go now," said Vera, with feigned impatience.

Veblen released her, mumbled an apology, and then picked up his everlux and pointed its long beam down the tunnel which stretched itself into the distance in either direction. As he examined the underground passageway, he decided that it was at least twenty meters wide, including a two and a half meter shelf on either side; more than enough room for a transport barge and a team of six-legged arixiaths which pulled them from one city to the next. The only sound inside the tunnel, besides their own heavy breathing, was the gurgle of water as it inexorably passed by.

"This passage is much larger than I thought it would be," exclaimed Vera. "This tunnel must run for hundreds of kilometers."

"Seker is honeycombed with these passages," said Veblen. "There is a complete latticework of them under all three continents. And what's even more astounding is that most of the work has been done by hand over many thousands and thousands of years, though they were helped by a profusion of caverns and caves underneath the planet's surface. In fact, Buzthara is located in a natural cavern of enormous size."

"I can't understand why they went to all that trouble to create an underground world? Seker is a pleasant planet, the gravity is close to earth standard, the surface is teeming with edible plant and animal life, and the climate is tolerable, though a touch on the hot side."

"The major reason that the Ophidians were forced to create their subterranean world," said Veblen, "is that Seker is continuously bombarded with high-frequency light radiations, because of its thin layer of ozone in the upper atmosphere. While these ultraviolet rays and other radiations are within acceptable limits for human tolerance, the Ophidians, with their super-sensitive eyes and heat sensors, find the surface intolerable for any length of time. Which is why only the Thadrons, or human nomads, live on the surface of Seker."

Pointing up toward the air duct from which they had just climbed down, Vera asked, "Why don't the Thadrons use these ducts to raid some of the smaller Ophidian towns and storage depots."

"The surface humans, that is those who live free of Ophidian control, take great care in not attracting attention to themselves. There are many Ophidians who are unaware that there are free human beings who exist on this planet. Seker was devoid of intelligent life when the Ophidians first landed about fifty thousand years ago. Apparently some of the human slaves were able to escape from their compounds on the surface, and over succeeding genera-

Hello Max.

The maximum 120mm cigarette.

Great tobaccos. Terrific taste.
And a long, lean,
__all-white__ dynamite look.

Menthol or Regular.

"Hello long, lean and delicious."

Regular: 17 mg. "tar," 1.3 mg. nicotine; Menthol: 18 mg. "tar," 1.3 mg. nicotine av. per cigarette by FTC Method.

MAX

MENTHOL 120's by KENT

FILTER 120's by KENT

Newport

Alive with pleasure!

Newport 20 CLASS A CIGARETTES

MENTHOL KINGS

17 mg. "tar", 1.2 mg. nicotine, av. per cigarette, FTC Report Apr. '75.

tions, banded together in small tribes. The Ophidians seem to be content to leave them alone as long as they don't upset the status quo, and even do a limited amount of trading with them through their human intermediaries. Occasionally, one of the more desperate bands will attack an Ophidian compound, but the Ophidians have discouraged these attacks over the years by making very punitive retaliatory raids—usually killing ten humans for every one of their own dead." Even in the poor light, Veblen could see the despair etched into Vera's face.

"I just can't understand how our government can stand back and observe these atrocities with cold indifference," cried Vera, her voice full of bitterness. "The persecution of the human slaves on Seker by their inhuman masters is an open wound on the body of humanity!"

"Vera, you're indulging in verbal propaganda, not straight fact, when you use loaded words like atrocity and persecution. In truth, the majority of human beings on Seker are treated with more kindness and respect by the Ophidians, than they are on other worlds by their fellow humans. At least here they're not imprisoned and murdered for their religious beliefs, or because of ideological disputes. Comparatively speaking, the treatment of humans on Seker is fair and just; it is carefully prescribed by tradition and the law. There are relatively few atrocities, as you call them, committed on Seker because it is to the advantage of both humans and Ophidians to live together in harmony."

"It's all politics," Vera said stubbornly. "You know as well as I do that people in the Protectorate don't live like that."

"True, but the Protectorate is only a very small part

of mankind. And I admit we live in a free and tolerant society; but that doesn't give us the right to force our way of life on another world or race of beings."

"If I hadn't already been acquainted with your Orthodox learnings, I might seriously be considering the possibility that you have become possessed by your Ophidian persona."

"Humph," Veblen grunted. He could see through Vera's attempt to manipulate him into an admission he didn't want to make. His political views and affiliations were his business and no one else's. Why was it that everytime he began to feel close to her, she brought up politics? Being an Historian, a storage bin for facts rather than a scientist, like himself, she failed to maintain a properly objective viewpoint when examining an alien culture. As he well knew, it took training and discipline to shed the blinders of ethnocentrism and xenophobia. Was he doomed to spend the rest of the expedition alienated from the only woman he could relate to on Seker because of this?

"I hear something," said Vera, jolting Veblen out of his reverie.

Listening carefully, he could hear the distant sound of unshod hooves striking the stone ledge as it reverberated through the tunnel. Veblen fired an improvised torch he had made on the surface out of some sticks and the cloth from his ripped sleeve. In the murky distance he could see the black silhouette of the arixiaths who were stamping towards them. Just as the massive animals pulled right up to them, he heard a loud curse, and the lead arixiath stopped less than five decimeters away. Holding up the feeble light, he just barely discerned the outline of the Ophidian standing at the front of the barge.

"Move to the side, so the beasts can pass," Yelled the bargeman.

Veblen threw a frown at Vera to cut off a tart reply. "Accept my most humble apologies, clansman, but my lad and I have been set upon by vandals and ask only for the privilege of a short ride to the capital," he yelled.

The bargeman paused for a moment and then answered, "I'd like to help you, but the freight is on a tight schedule."

Veblen held up his purse and cried, "I'll make it well worth your while, clansman."

"Aye," he returned. "Place the plank, we have passengers coming aboard."

After nervously passing the six-legged arixiaths, who were half again his height, Veblen led Vera across the undersized plank and onto the barge. Then he haggled with the bargeman until they worked out an equitable price for their passage. He dropped two red, three yellow, and one white sequin into the Ophidian's hand.

During most of the voyage, Veblen and Vera were ignored by the Ophidian crew as they went about their work. The two investigators used this time to rest up from their trek across the surface of Seker, and to get a feel for the people they would be working with during the next few months. Twice their canal barge was passed by barges leaving Buzthara, and once by a single-person kayak. Veblen then explained to Vera how the kayaks were used to keep mail and official information flowing through the underground complex of cities and outposts.

As they approached Buzthara, they both noticed that their vision was becoming much stronger because of the slight glow radiating from the walls of the subterranean waterway. This faint phosphorescence was the major light source within Buzthara, and provided sufficient illumination for Ophidian eyes—although most humans were forced to live in a perpetual twilight world. This natural lighting was the primary reason that Buzthara had become both the planet's capitol and major administrative center.

"What causes the lighting?" asked Vera, as the barge left the tunnel and entered into the giant cavern, continuing to glide through the small harbor which was fed by a series of passageways similar to the one they had just left.

"It's a fungus which grows along the walls and roof of this cavern," said Veblen. "It grows on a couple of other caves and caverns on Seker, but none as large as this one."

"Why don't they transplant it then?"

"They have tried a number of times, but apparently there is a mineral or something else they need to survive that only occurs in this cavern and a few other places. The Ophidian science isn't advanced enough for them to conduct pH tests and rock-composition studies."

While the barge moved towards the wharves, which jutted out from the waterfront like jagged teeth, Veblen peered into the yellow haze and tried to get a good glimpse of the city. He was surprised by how dim and grey Buzthara looked until he remembered that the images stored in his mind had been made by Ophidian eyes, which were much more sensitive to glow from above.

As the barge pulled up to the docks, Veblen was able to get a much better view of the stone and clay subterranean city. While the cavern itself was enormous, the city took up its entire floor and cubical clay apartments climbed its walls. From where the barge was being moored, Veblen could see the squat warehouses and storehouses that crowded the docks; in the background, he could see the distant silhouettes of the great clan centers, the university, the hatchery, and the tip of the Temple of Set.

Once the barge had been made fast, they thanked the laconic barge tender and went on shore. Since it was far too late to contact their Informant at the prearranged meeting place, they decided to find an inn that catered to human clientele. With Vera two steps behind and her face covered, as was the custom, they left the busy waterfront area and began to walk towards the commercial center. Along with the stores and shops that lined the street, there were a few humans in this part of town, and they showed much less variety than the human food markets; the Ophidians were carnivores and looked upon grains and vegetables with great distaste. Growing hungrier and hungrier, since it had been a long time since their last meal, they stopped at one of the human food stalls and bought two loaves of unleavened bread which had been dipped into a tangy sauce and left to harden. The food was good, and if it hadn't been for their physical discomfort, they both would have enjoyed their walk through the streets of Buzthara.

"Where are we going to find a place to stay?" asked Vera, as they entered an area of the city where the shops and stores were diminishing, replaced by large and imposing stone buildings. Most of the people who moved down the narrow street were the multi-colored Ophidians, and there were almost no women, Ophidian or human. It was obvious that Vera's disordered appearance was beginning to attract attention to them.

"Few humans live on this side of the city," answered Veblen sotto voce, trying not to attract any more attention. "So I don't think there's much chance of finding any accommodations until we reach Stinktown."

"Stinktown!"

"That's the unofficial name for the human ghetto in Buzthara, though its use is condemned by the more progressive Ophidians. However, from an Ophidian point of view, the name, while graphic, is aromatically correct."

As they drew closer to the center of the city they found that the narrow streets were beginning to overflow with Ophidians of every description. They almost had to push their way through the crowd to make any progress at all. Coming upon a fellow human, whose pedcab had been brought to a halt by the milling throng, Veblen asked him the reason for the large crowd. After giving him a puzzled look, the man told him that today happened to be the first day of celebration of the Festival of Serpents.

Several minutes later—after having just managed to avoid a careening wagon, tearing through the streets as though they were empty—Vera asked, "Wouldn't it be easier if we tried to avoid the festival by going around it?"

"I don't think so," answered Veblen, "Taipan Street leads right through Temple Plaza and directly into the human enclave. Any other route would mean a long detour and a great deal of unnecessary walking.

Vera sighed loudly but did not contest his decision, being no less foot-weary than the Investigator.

Another ten minutes of squeezing and pushing brought them to the foot of Temple Plaza, which was overflowing with merry makers and revellers. At one end of the block-sized square squatted the University of Jarazia, which resembled a great stone fortress; while at the opposite side, towered the Temple of Set, a lofty ziggurat which dominated the southern skyline. Near the center of the plaza was a large stage covered with dancing Ophidian women in bright-colored clothing.

As he stared at the gyrating dancers, he began to push through the crowd to get closer to the stage. Although flat-chested, the Ophidian dancers were endowed with lithe figures and moved with grace and elegance. Their sinuous movements were erotic and exciting and Veblen felt his blood begin to warm. They began the final movements in the *Dance of the Andromeda Flight,* and he caught sight of a statuesque green-skinned beauty who set his heart to pounding. A bouquet of turquoise and black plumes crowned her head, while her lower limbs were pleasingly displayed by diaphanous pink pants.

"Are we just going to stand here all day while you ogle these half-naked snake-women?" asked Vera snappishly.

"I was merly evaluating their performance of the *Dance of the Andromeda Flight.* It is one of the oldest and most important dances, traditionally speaking. It symbolically recreates the Ophidian exodus from their home galaxy and their final escape from the Trisaurian's Great Search." Veblen heard Vera's short gasp and asked, "What is it?"

"Look over there!" scried Vera.

He turned and looked into the crowd seeing nothing unusual. Leaning towards her, he asked, "What did you see?"

"I'm almost certain I saw a man wearing the purple robes of the Order of Universal Symmetry."

"Well, whoever it was, he's gone now," said Veblen.

Was it possible that the Brotherhood was on Seker, or was Vera mistaken? After all, there were dozens of brightly-robed figures all around them. It looked like he had yet another mystery to mull over. That wasn't quite what he needed right now, he thought, as he let his eyes feast on the provocative Ophidian dancers. He felt himself tremble as one of the dancers exposed her bare chest and decided that it was more than breasts that made the female torso so stimulating; there was the curve of the waist, the flair of the hips, and the slight bulge of the belly. He turned and studied Vera's figure as she stood watching the dancers, and decided that her body was as attractive as any of the Ophidians dancing on the stage. Maybe even more so, he thought, as his eyes lingered on her well-rounded breasts. If only they had gotten along better; after all, they were going to be spending a lot of time together on this mission. But then, he thought ruefully, he should have thought of that a long time ago.

Nine

"Furthermore," charged the Master Magus, before the assembly of Elders in the Council Hall, "the First Elder did willfully conspire with the off-worlders, granting them permission to establish a base on Seker in the Royd Mountains, for concessions, as of yet, undetermined. By so doing, not only has he misused the powers invested in him by the Covenant, but he has broken his oath of office and usurped the authority of this Council. I formally charge him with abuse of power and failure to abide by the rules and regulations as set forth in the Covenant. I ask that he be shorn of his cloak of office, that his staff be broken in two, and that he be removed, forcibly if necessary, from the Council Hall and that those Counsellors and ministers who assisted him be treated likewise."

The Master Magus took his seat in the shocked silence that followed his charges and hoped that he had not overdone it. He had decided earlier that by calling forth the maximum charges, he might be able to shock the Council into censuring the First Elder at the very least. By the angry buzz of conversation beginning to spread through the benches, he knew that he had accomplished his first objective and that his motions would not be silently shelved.

As the hall fell quiet, the First Elder rose to his feet, smiled graciously at the Master Magus, and let his sibilant voice fill the hall. "Fellow Elders. As much as it pains me to say this, I must agree that the Master's charges are substantively true. . . ."

The full Council hissed like an angry serpent.

The Master Magus stared at the First Elder in disbelief. What stratagem, he wondered, was behind this unexpected admission of guilt?

"However," stormed the First Elder, his voice lashing out like a whip, "my actions were in full accord with a higher and much greater law."

He had everyone's full attention.

"Too many of our people have become corrupted and have turned their backs on the old ways." Pointing an accusing finger at the Master Magus, he added, "And then there are those who conspire to change our laws and our traditions to favor their human minions and their own personal aggrandizement. I now openly denounce them and their tools. It is time we return to the ways of our ancestors and throw off the shackles they have forged with their false laws and Covenant. Let us once again follow the trail of the Great Serpent and regain our former glory and pride."

Aware of many hostile looks now directed his way, the Master Magus wondered just how much the university had underestimated the power and strength of Old Religion. That it was still taught in the clan crèches, was well known, but they had evidently disregarded its influence. Now they all might have to pay for this mistake of miscalculation.

"We all have a sacred obligation to the laws of He who fathered the First Egg. The Prophecy has been fulfilled and it is now time for these of the True Faith to make their courage known. The laws of the clans are but shadows before the laws of the Great Serpent. It is for you to decide the destiny of all Ophidians, present and future."

The First Elder stood silent. The Elder, who was presiding over this special session of the Council, asked, "Do you have anything further to say in your defense?"

"Yes, I would like to call the High Priest of Set before the Council to speak in my defense."

Moments later, the High Priest entered the hall from the anteroom where he had obviously been waiting for this summons. He strutted in resplendent glory, his gold and vermillion robes trailing down to the granite floor. Upon his head he wore a jewel-encrusted miter, which blazed forth in rainbow bursts each time he passed one of the slowly burning tapers set into the walls. In his right hand he carried a silver rod, which at the tip was formed into a snake's head, with bared fangs gleaming wickedly. All the Elders watched with wonder as this awe-striking figure, the ecclesiastical head of a church which had seen its apex a hundred thousand years before, walked to the front of the Council Hall.

"Brothers of the True Race," began the High Priest, "the time has come for us to return to the old ways."

The Master Magus looked around himself at the spellbound faces and saw the beginning of the end to a great dream. The Magi had not only failed to reach the people, but had completely underestimated their opposition to the path of peaceful progress.

The High Priest held up a piece of yellowed parchment and claimed in a booming voice, "At long last the Prophecy has been answered. It is all here in the *Song of the Serpent*.

"When the sky-bird comes and lands near the
   crèche,
All must relearn from the few who can teach.
In the big nest where all the clans gather,
The storm that comes will be sky-bird weather.
As sure as the Great Serpent sheds his skin,
The True Race will know the cosmos again."

"The sky-birds have landed and the Prophecy has come true," cried the High Priest, his voice shaking the walls. "It is up to us now to tear off the chains that bind us to this underworld life and fly free through the universe. We shall scour the worlds of man, and once again they shall know the touch of our whips. We are the Chosen. If we but have faith in our Creator, we shall win. It is time for all the True Race to join together and destroy our vile enemies."

A ragged cheer ripped through the hall and the Master Magus slumped back in his bench in despair. He saw the fistfight break out in the front of the hall and shook his head in disbelief. If only they could see themselves, he thought, as he watched dignified statesmen screaming abuse at each other. They are behaving worse than the humans they profess to despise so much. If this was how the city's wisest and most respected leaders acted, how would the workers and tenders of Buzthara's streets respond? His whole body felt weak; it was as though an earthquake had shaken the bedrock of his beliefs.

The presiding Elder began to strike a gong to restore order, but its sound was lost in the thunder of argument. "Order! Order!" he cried.

The clamor continued for several more minutes before it died away to an angry murmur. The presiding Elder waited for complete quiet and then asked for a vote of confidence. As over two-thirds of the Elder Council voted their support of the First Elder and his policies, the Master Magus sat stunned. Elders who had voted against the First Elder were openly reviled as traitors and damned souls.

Where would it all end, the Master Magus asked himself, as he watched the Elders slowly leave the hall. They were mad to think they could defy the universe. Where was the sanity and levelheadedness of his youth? Was the university to die in one last orgy of fire and destruction? Where would the First Elder's mad quest for power lead them? The future of Seker and the Ophidian race was in the hands of the university.

When he finally rose to his feet, the Master Magus stood stooped and bent, weighed down by the heavy hand of time and care.

Ten

"YOU MIGHT AS WELL GO ahead and eat," said the Informant, a plain-looking man with a sallow complexion, who was called Pol. "Jarl won't be here for at least another hour."

With resignation, Veblen looked down at the five or six flatcakes, covered with an unappetizing chutney, and decided that he had better start getting used to the local foods. He took another sip of tieaf, a bitter-tasting dark green brew, and began to eat one of the flatcakes that appeared to be relatively free of the spicy sienna-colored sauce.

After an uneventful three days in Buzthara, Veblen was beginning to feel restless and he was anxious to meet Jarl, the Informant who had infiltrated the University of Jarazia. He and Vera had found little difficulty finding lodgings for the night, once they had reached the human ghetto, and they had spent the next day locating their contact man, Pol. Since then, they had been living in their Informant's clay-walled house, waiting while he contacted Jarl. During this time, they had learned little of value and Veblen was beginning to regard the small house as a prison of sorts.

When he and Vera had finished as much of their breakfast as they dared, the Informant's wife had cleared the table and had brought them fresh cups of tieaf. As he sipped the dark green liquid, Veblen began to mull over the unanswered question which clogged his mind like tangled webs. Where had the spaceships come from? Who had brought them to Seker? Why were they such a well-guarded secret? What were they going to be used for? Where were they hidden? Thoughts and ideas cartwheeled through his head, but they refused to form any meaningful pattern and he began to feel a sharp pain at the back of his skull.

A loud knock on the door startled him and he reached underneath his shirt to grasp the handle of the laser he had hidden there.

Pol walked cautiously up to the wooden door and asked, "Who is it?"

"Jarl," rasped a voice in answer.

Pol opened the door and in walked a large man wearing a floor-length green cloak bordered in yellow. Jarl was stout, with a rounded belly that made one think that his chest had dropped about a meter. His face was massive and looked as though someone had taken two lumps of plaster and slapped them on either side, and then stuck a red-veined turnip in the center. Two bush-like eyebrows formed a roof over the cavern where his eyes burned like distant fires.

"Jarl," said Pol, "I'd like you to meet Investigator Thorstein Veblen."

Veblen offered a greeting and found himself under exacting scrutiny for almost a minute. He felt like a biological specimen on a cutting board, and it took an exercise in will to keep a fixed gaze on the other man.

"You're new, aren't you?" asked Jarl, managing to make his question sound like an accusation.

"This is my first case," answered Veblen.

Jarl banged his fist down on the thick wooden table with a sound like that of a slamming door. "Damn it," he stormed, "I asked them to send an experienced and capable man for this mission and look what I get!"

Veblen felt as though the temperature of the room had just gone up ten degrees. He forced himself to remain quiet; he was neither going to apologize for his presence nor lose his temper.

"Calm down," cried Pol. "The Bureau knows how important this mission is and I'm sure they sent the best man they had available."

Jarl didn't seem to be very convinced and he yanked off his cloak revealing the saffron robe he wore underneath.

Still trying to clear the air, Pol turned to the two Investigators and said, "I don't know how much the Bureau told you, but Jarl is the man who discovered that the Ophidians had been in contact with outsiders and given several interplanetary craft."

"We didn't know that," said Vera.

"What is she doing here?" demanded Jarl, as though he was noticing her for the very first time.

"Vera is my assistant," stated Veblen, in a no-nonsense tone of voice, "and she is quite capable of handling her job."

Vera flashed him a warm smile.

Jarl groaned and dropped his face into his open hands.

Pol continued as though there had never been an interruption. "Jarl has been very successful on Seker. He was the third human to ever become a Magus, and has made many contributions to our understanding of Ophidian culture." Then, with almost paternal pride, he added, "But then you would expect a great deal from a Fifth Level Sociologist who has dedicated himself to a lifetime study of the Ophidian culture and society."

Fifth Level, thought Veblen, with surprise, He was impressed. Most of those who reached that remote plateau became planetary representatives in the Anomian League as members of the Supreme Committee and spent the rest of their days on Anomia; rarely ever leaving, even to visit the worlds they were supposedly representing.

"Enough of your eulogizing," said Jarl. Turning to Veblen he asked, "What is your plan of action, Investigator?"

Right then, Veblen wanted more than anything else to be able to come up with a clear and concise plan of action; but it wasn't happening. "I really don't have any plan at all, right now. I was hoping for some new information that might clear things up a little."

"That's what I was afraid of," said the Informant, with more resignation than rancor this time. "But at least you're honest. I have given it some thought and, if I were in your shoes, I wouldn't know where to start either. What do you need to know?"

After some careful thought, since Veblen knew that any mistake or error in judgment that he made would be concisely recorded for all those who might be interested, he spoke. "I would like to know how you found out about the fact that these ships had been brought to Seker?"

Briefly, Jarl told him how the First Elder had announced the arrival of the off-worlders to his clan, and how, as proof of their friendship, they had presented the Ophidians with three interplanetary vessels. Furthermore, the First Elder had claimed, that the off-worlders wanted to form an alliance with the Ophidians to help them throw off the invisible shackles of the Anomian Protectorate—promising them deliveries of interstellar spacecraft and advanced weaponry to do so.

"Then the Ophidians know that we watch over them?" asked Vera.

"They have known it for a long time," said Jarl. "There are a number of telepathic sensitives, and it doesn't seem farfetched that one of them might have made contact with one of our Informants."

"Since all of the 'gifted' reside in the university," said Veblen, "how is it that they haven't discovered your role."

"Because all the 'gifted' are kept in the sanctuary, and are isolated from all but a very few ministers and Magi, selected by the Master Magus himself. You must remember that the Ophidians look upon their 'gifted' as almost sacred beings who hold the future of the race in their genes. The university has been entrusted with their care and development; a job which they take very seriously."

"How do they feel about our presence?"

"It is not a well-known fact. There are those at the university who, because of our policy of nonintervention, view us as friendly observers; while, on the other hand, there are those who see our presence as a deadly insult. It has the potential for being a very volatile political issue."

"Have the off-worlders made any attempt to land on Seker?" asked Veblen.

"Yes, it was recently learned by one of the Brethren, who passed the information on to the Master, that the off-worlders have established a base on Seker just north of Zendo, in the foothills of the Royd Mountains. Therefore, it seems to me," he added, "that your most logical move would be to travel to the Royd Mountains and investigate the outsiders' camp yourselves."

"How long would that take?"

"A couple of hours using your ship. By kayak it would take a week."

"Not our ship," said Veblen. "Our craft was sabotaged and most of our equipment was a total loss. We were lucky to have escaped with our lives."

"I don't believe this," exclaimed Jarl, waving his hands in the air. "What is the Bureau of Extraterrestrial Investigations trying to do? Set us back a thousand years!"

Veblen ignored Jarl's outburst. "The simplest solution is not necessarily the wisest. I don't think that a trip to the Royd Mountains would help us much at all. We would probably just end up walking into a trap —I'm sure the off-worlders are expecting us to show up sooner or later. Besides, I think that most of the action is going to be right here in Buzthara."

"What gives you that idea?" said Jarl, scornfully.

"For some reason, I just don't think that the outsiders have taken what they really came here for in the first place. All they have done so far is give away a couple of their ships and establish a small base. To tell you the truth, I just can't believe that they actually plan to use Seker as some sort of Trojan horse against the Protectorate."

"The Ophidians are savage fighters," countered Jarl. "They are remembered with fear and disgust throughout the worlds of man, which gives them a tremendous psychological edge. Furthermore, they could geometrically increase the size of their population overnight. A female Ophidian goes into oestrus four times a year, and ovulates whether or not she has been fertilized. Each fertilized egg incubates in four to five months, so, theoretically, the Ophidian population could double on one year and grow in great leaps every year thereafter."

"Even so," said Veblen, "the Ophidians have no real technology and therefore would be totally dependent upon their allies for spaceships and armaments—which, on top of everything else, would have to be brought through our patrols before they could arrive on Seker. Moreover, there isn't a highly developed civilization that the Ophidians could pillage within a hundred light years. As the Revisionists are so fond of reminding us, the Protectorate is primarily an area of underdeveloped and technologically backward worlds. No, if we're going to come under attack, it's not going to be from within; but from the outside."

"Then why do you think the outsiders have landed here," asked Jarl disdainfully.

"I don't know," answered Veblen, "but I mean to find out."

"But where are you going to start?" asked Pol.

"To begin with," said Veblen, pausing to take a sip of tieaf, "I thought I would visit the university and have a talk with the Master Magus and see what he thinks."

"I can tell you right now," said Jarl, "there's nothing that he can tell you, that I can't."

"You may be right Jarl, but right now I'm not searching for more information, I'm looking for allies. And it seems to me that the Magi are as firmly opposed to the off-worlders as we are ourselves."

"True," nodded Jarl, grudgingly.

"Therefore, it appears to me that it would be to our advantage to work with the Magi and share information with them on the basis of equality, rather than having to rely on your continued success."

"You have a good point," said Jarl, his eyes giving Veblen a careful reappraisal.

"Also," said Veblen, "there is a lot more I would like to learn about these 'gifted' Ophidians and some of the cults that have sprung up recently, like the Mambas and the Cobra Cult."

"Where did you hear about them!" Jarl asked.

"Thorstein's persona was from an Ophidian," said Vera.

"I didn't know it was possible for a man to survive such a memory transfer without permanent psychological damage," said Jarl, as he looked at Veblen with guarded respect.

"I didn't either," added Pol.

"There were some rather unpleasant side effects," said Veblen, "but my Ophidian persona has already proven its worth several times."

"Some time in the future," stated Jarl, with a grimace that was intended to be friendly, "when matters are less urgent, we will have to discuss Ophidian psychology and customs in some detail."

"It should prove enlightening for both of us, I'm sure, but what else can you tell me about the psionic research the Magi have been conducting?"

"It is part of their long-range design, the Great Plan as they call it, to bring forth all the latent potential of both humans and Ophidians. It is one of their tenets that war and conquest will not bring greatness or continued survival for the Ophidians. They believe that if the Ophidians can prove that they can live harmoniously with humans, they will be much more successful and prosperous than their ancestors. In order for this to happen, they feel that the Ophidians have to offer a unique service to mankind, so they have been encouraging and guiding the psychological and parapsychological development of their own race through selective breeding and eugenics."

"How successful have they been?"

"There are maybe a hundred and twenty-five of the 'gifted' within the university, but their abilities and true location are known only to the Master Magus and his ministers. I have heard it rumored that some of the 'gifted' are capable of precognition, telekinesis, and mind reading; but what is fact and what is fiction, I do not know."

"I think I should pay the Master Magus a visit as soon as it is possible. Can it be arranged?"

Jarl looked down at the floor for a moment and then said, "Yes, I think a meeting can be set up . . . though it will mean breaking my cover. But I guess that isn't important any more. At least I hope not . . . there's so much more to be learned here." Then, as though having made some inner decision, he said firmly, "I'll return to the university right away and send you a messenger tomorrow telling you when you are to appear."

Eleven

HAD THE PROCTOR STILL been subject to emotional responses, he would have described himself as angry; but even his memories of such dysfunctional states had faded into obscurity, and he had to settle for agitated. His brain was no more the highly disorganized and reactive pulp he had been born with than his body was the weak organic shell he had been condemned with at birth. When he had undergone his Conversion, a lengthy series of major operations and implants, his body had been strengthened and rejuvenated; his mind had been improved by electronic amplifiers and information implants. Furthermore, all the neural nexuses for emotional responses, and their feedback loops, had been removed from his brain along with the corresponding parts of the limbic system and the hypothalamus. His body had been purged of its unnecessary sense of smell by the elimination of the olfactory nerve; the facial and glossopharyngeal nerves for taste; and the gonads, which were responsible for the production of sexual hormones—plus the sexual regulators within the hypothalamus, pituitary gland, and also the pineal gland.

After the operations had been successfully completed, he had then spent six months in a sensory deprivation tank so he could learn to detach himself from his body and to see if he had achieved the proper state of grace. Once he had proven his mind superior to its prison of flesh, he had spent five years in a monastery meditating and studying the Unor, the Order's bible and master plan for the human race. When this five-year period ended, and his penance had been completed, the Prime Monitor had judged him pure.

One out of every three of the Brothers who underwent Conversion was found to be lacking in faith and purity, which was demonstrated by a display of deviant behavior such as a weapon fetish, an outburst of homicidal mania, a pain perversion, an attempt at suicide, or an enjoyment of self-mutilation—almost all of which were centered around pain—the strongest and most important of their remaining senses. For the Proctor to have been found eligible for elevation to the Elect, or *homo machina* was a profound honor.

However, in spite of what the lays and Brothers thought, being a member of the Elect did not mean that one was above reproach—as he had just been reminded by a Tachyon beam transmission from Capek, the artificial planetoid which contained the mental nucleus of the Prime Monitor, castigating him for his lack of success. The Order of Universal Symmetry tolerated little in the way of inefficiency or delay, and he knew that failure in this mission could lead to his exile on some backwater world as an observer, where he would stay until the Prime Monitor was satisfied that he had paid his penance.

Already Operation Psi was weeks behind schedule,

and he was beginning to wonder what excuses Brother Bernard would have this time for not completing his assignment. Where was that pie-faced moron, he asked himself; he had sent out a recall order hours ago. The Brother should have returned to the ship by now. Why had they given him such inept help on such an important mission? The man was more emotional than a recently converted lay and not much brighter than a Guardian. When he had worn the purple robes, such a man would have been defrocked and his brain would have been added to the Prime Monitor's bionic core. He would have a long talk with his superiors when he returned to Capek. The last time they had talked, he had been forced to take a supportive role just to keep the Brother from breaking down into hysterics. If he hadn't needed the Brother as a liaison man with the Ophidians, he would have discharged him and placed him in one of the cryrogenic tanks for the rest of the mission.

Hearing the musical tones of the Heraldkey, the Proctor pressed the button that opened the cabin door. In walked Brother Bernard, with his shoulders slumped and a dejected expression on his wide face. The word disgust took on a new intellectual dimension for the Proctor as he watched the Brother slide into the contour body-seat, which had to expand far beyond its designer's intent to greet the Brother's girth.

"The weapons were delivered without incident. Weren't they?"

"Yes, Proctor, as I told you in my last dispatch," answered Brother Bernard listlessly. "The First Elder claims that he was successfully able to maintain the Council's support."

"Then what is wrong?"

"I just received some bad news from one of our

operatives, which is why it took me so long to answer your summons."

"Yes. I understand," said the Proctor, "please continue."

"Anyway, the operative told me that an Anomian Investigator and his assistant have arrived on Seker."

The Proctor realized that the statistical anomaly to the laws of probability—that most men referred to as luck—had just run out. Originally, before the battle with the Anomian Navy, and their loss of three ships and the damage to *The Sword of Wrath's* reaction drive, he had hoped to have completed his mission long before the Anomian Bureau of Extraterrestrial Investigations had sufficient time to send an Investigator to the planet Seker. But now, like everything else on the ill-begotten mission, that too had gone awry. "We will have to do something about that," said the Proctor, thoughtfully.

"Possibly," answered the Brother, "but I've run into a snag in Operation Psi."

"What's that?"

"I haven't been able to find a way to gain entrance to the university. I can't abduct the sensitives that we've been ordered to bring back to Capek."

"I thought we had an operative inside the university! After all, I've paid out a small fortune for one."

"I know," said the Brother dishearteningly, "but the Magi keep the 'gifted,' as they call their psychic sensitives, secreted in a citadel deep in the heart of the university, which is a solid stone stronghold. Only a Master Magus, his ministers, and a small supportive staff are ever allowed inside. The Ophidians look upon the 'gifted' as a genetic treasure to be guarded and nurtured for the good of the race."

"As well they should."

"I agree, yet because of the difficulty in obtaining entrance into this citadel, our operative has been unable to help us abduct them."

"We have been here for over a month, Brother, while you have conducted negotiations with the First Elder for an alliance, and then permission to mine the radioactive ore we need. But somewhere along the line you have evidently forgotten why we are here and what our mission is. All this means nothing if we do not bring several of these telepaths back to Capek for examination by the Prime Monitor. If the Order can learn just what alignment of chromosomal DNA is responsible for these particular abilities, no power in the universe will be able to stop us. The Brotherhood will become the only church, and our Order the only state. This is why it is imperative that we succeed."

"I realize this," answered the Brother, his fat face covered with small droplets of perspiration.

"Good," said the Proctor, "I want you to concentrate all your energy into removing those telepaths, and I don't care if you have to start a war to do it!"

"If it would help any," said Brother Bernard, his voice quivering, "I would start one tomorrow. However, the First Elder's power is secure and there is nothing I can use that would force him to make so dangerous a move as attacking the university. The University of Jarazia is a sanctuary that is held inviolable. If anything, the Ophidians have more respect, and a greater sense of propriety, for their sacred institutions than we humans. Such an act would not only be personally abhorrent to the First Elder, but, as he is well aware, would bring the wrath of the populace down upon him. The only reason he has formed an alliance with us is that we have promised

107

to aid him in restoring the Ophidians to their former glory. So, in a sense, he is fighting more for a restoration of the old ways—in the face of an industrial upheaval brought about by the Magi—than just for any desire to gain power on his own. . . ."

"I understand all of this, Brother," said the Proctor impatiently. He wondered if it might not be a good idea to jettison the garrulous Brother out one of the airlocks, without a spacesuit, once the mission was over. "Is your mind so atrophic," he continued, "that you can think of only one or two solutions to your problems?"

The Brother cringed as though he had been struck, and the Proctor decided that he had better give him some reassurance before his neurosis incapacitated him completely. "Calm yourself, Brother. I will help you find the necessary path," said the Proctor. "After the successful conclusion of this assignment, I can promise you that you will find true serenity." Seeing the smile that crossed the Brother's face, he thought to himself. You will find the peace you seek, though it may be more than you expect.

"Unfortunately," resumed the Proctor, "we don't have nearly enough operatives to storm the university, even with lasers."

"If only the ship hadn't been damaged," blurted the Brother. "We could fly . . . well, I guess we couldn't."

The Proctor made a beatific smile, but inwardly considered the man an overemotional reject from the breeder colonies. If he hadn't known it was theoretically impossible, he might believe that he was starting to hate that lump of lard. "If the Ophidians lived on the surface," began the Proctor in a neutral tone, "like any other civilized people, we could take our time, fix the ship, bull our way into the university,

and take those sensitives of
practically inaccessible, we a
up a new approach."

"Maybe I could give the F
tion which would lead him to
tend to push him from power.

"Too obvious," said the P
idea with a frown. "Do you h
records of these 'gifted'?"

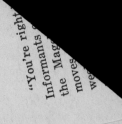

"No, but I'm sure I could obta⸱⸱ ⸱⸱em from one of
our operatives. These Ophidians keep track of their
ancestrial bloodlines like the ancient Terrans used to
do with their favorite pets and plants. What do you
want their genealogies for?"

"Just an idea," the Proctor said. "I'll tell you more
about it after I've given it some more study."

"What happened at the special Council session?"
asked Veblen.

"The First Elder not only admitted that he had
broken several of the Covenant's laws, but asked them
to reward him for doing it," said the Master Magus.

"How did the Council react?"

"They stood up and cheered, as though they were
in the stands watching the combat rituals in the Pit.
It certainly brought an end to the last of my illusions
about how successful the university has been in
combating superstition and ignorance. That's not to
say that there wasn't any opposition to him, but he
obviously won over the majority of the Council—and
had his opposition branded as traitors and turncoats.
And now it seems that the people of Buzthara are
completely behind him, at least for now. If the First
Elder is allowed to continue in this insane crusade, it
could truly destroy us all."

," said Veblen. "The Protectorate has
—n Seker, and every non-League world in
—llanics. If your people made any hostile
—, there would be a fleet out here within a few
—ks and any uprising would be handled with the
utmost severity. The Protectorate's policies are under
attack both at home and from the outside, and such
an uprising might threaten its very existence. It
would be a costly move for everyone involved."

"Maybe that is why the off-worlders have formed
an alliance with us?"

"I don't know," said Veblen. "There are many
possible reasons, though I don't see how an Anomian
change in government would help any of our enemies.
I would think they would want to avoid it, since the
Revisionists are much more militant than the Orthodoxy has ever been. In fact, there may not be any
outsiders; this whole thing may possibly be a deft
political move by the Revisionist Party to discredit
the Orthodox Party's complete platform, and bring
themselves into power. Or possibly it's just a ploy by
the off-worlders to take your attention off what they
really came after. On the other hand, it may be an
attempt to draw part of the Anomian Naval forces
away from their normal patrols, so they can soften
our defenses for an attack. No matter what the reason, it will be your people who will suffer the most."

"That is what I was afraid of," said the Master
Magus somberly. "I'm only glad that now I have an
ally."

Some ally, thought Veblen, as his mind assessed his
current difficulties: his wrecked ship, his lack of
knowledge, and his inability to find any clues.

"I have confidence," continued the Master Magus,
"that with your help we shall stop the off-worlders

and their Ophidian confederates before they have hatched their deadly plans."

Veblen carefully studied the saffron-robed Ophidian. His face was colored a deep red which ended at the neck, where there was a black and then a white band which disappeared underneath the yellow of his garment. Except for the diamond patterns which covered his skin, the absence of any hair, and the small triangular pits underneath each elliptical eye, his features were not very different from those of a human being. Every inch of the Master Magus showed strength and granite-like resolve. Veblen decided that if anyone was capable of pulling the Ophidians back from the edge of the abyss they trod so daringly, that it was this Magus who had dedicated himself to his people.

"Could you tell me," Veblen asked, trying to make some sort of coherent pattern out of the disarray of data within his mind, "if the man who saw the off-worlders base, saw them doing anything out of the usual?"

"He claimed that they were using metal beasts to chew up the ground," answered the Master Magus. "Does that help?"

"Maybe. I'm almost certain they're not here for any kind of mining operation, not in the center of hostile territory. So it is possible that they're low on fuel. It must be their reaction drive. It uses radioactives that could easily be found on any earth-type planet."

"What is this reaction drive?"

"Do you know anything abut atomic power and the Theory of Relativity?"

"Yes," replied the Master Magus. "While our culture is not very advanced in a technological sense, we still have reproductions of many of the information cassettes and books that were brought to Seker by our ancestors. Much of that information has been preserved and studied within the university; after all, we are responsible for the future of our race and we take this obligation very seriously."

"Fine," Veblen said. "The reaction drive is a means of propulsion based on the use of controlled atomic fission. Since it is a *real* universe drive—that is subject to the Einsteinian laws—it is not capable of passing the light barrier of two hundred and ninety-seven thousand kilometers per second. At such low speeds, interstellar travel is impractical if not impossible. But such speeds are sufficient to propel a spaceship out beyond the pull of any nearby stellar bodies, allowing the use of the Stromborg Shift, which circumvents the limitations of relativity by making a jump, so to speak, into another dimension. Therefore, it is my guess that the off-worlders have either run low on their radioactive fuel, or have had some type of accident that has diminished their supply—enough so that their ship is incapable of leaving this solar system, or being able to use their Stomborg Shift safely."

"But if all the off-wolders needed was fuel for their reaction drive," asked the Magus, with a puzzled frown, "why did they bother to interfere in our politics?"

"I think their fuel situation is just incidental to whatever brought them to Seker. What we need to discover is who they are and what brought them here."

"That makes sense," said the Master Magus. "If what has taken place so far is just a sample, then their plans may have catastrophic consequences for us all. I will have several of the 'gifted' make mind-

112

contact with some of our agents in Zendo and have them see what they can learn about the off-wolders and their base."

"That will be a good start. If we could learn the identity of the off-worlders, we might find a clue as to what they came here for."

"Now, as I see it, our next real problem is to find a way to stop the First Elder before he consolidates his position and declares himself Oligarch."

"He must have some enemies?"

"We have already checked this out," the Master Magus said, "since we were sure that not all of the tribes in the Viperidae Clan would be pleased to see their power usurped by the Cerastes Tribe. The official leadership of Seker is rotated every four years between the tribes of the Viperidae Clan, which is the traditional ruling clan on our world. The Bitis Tribe, which is supposed to assume the rule next spring, is extremely disturbed by the First Elder's maneuvers and has already pledged its support to the university. However, the Viperea Tribe appears to be already committed to the First Elder. The Atheris Tribe is walking the edge of a shell and refuses to declare its support for either side."

"What about the other clans—how do they feel about the Elder's rise to power?"

"He has much more support than I would have believed possible a month ago. The majority of tribes in both the Colubrinae Clan and the Hydrophidae Clan—which are the two clans whose members feel most threatened by the recent industrialization—fully support the First Elder and his policies. Fortunately, the Boidae Clan, which provides the majority of guards and soldiers, is divided in its support of the First Elder; although it appears that General Gallon, commander of the Blue Regiment, has already decided in his favor. We have managed to win the support of two tribes in the Elapidae Clan, but we don't have the strength to stop him.

"What we need is a change in public opinion," said Veblen thoughtfully. "And some way to spread our message to the people of Buzthara. How about some kind of rumor control agency with operatives to direct the city's flow of information by starting some rumors and killing others. During periods of political upheaval, people are willing to believe almost anything and if we can control what they hear. . . ."

A loud knock sounded on the door and they both looked up in surprise. "Come in," cried the Master Magus.

What calamity was upon them now, thought Veblen as his heart pounded against his chest. Had the First Elder made his move already? His mouth almost dropped open as Jarl, the Anomian Informant and human Magus, walked into the room.

"What is it?" demanded the Master Magus, in a tone that made it clear that there had better be a good reason for disturbing his privacy.

Jarl turned toward Veblen. "I have an important message for Investigator Veblen." He paused dramatically, and then added, "It seems that Vera, your assistant, has been kidnapped."

Twelve

"CAPTAIN! WHAT IS THE meaning of this intrusion?"
cried the First Elder, as he nodded to his Pythoninae
guard to cover the soldier from behind in case this was
an assassination attempt. During the past week, his
control over the city had increased daily as tribe after
tribe had rallied to his support. Yesterday, the Atheris
Tribe had sent its Elders to his chamber to offer their
allegiance, and he was aware that his adversaries had
their backs to the wall. It was quite possible that they
might have decided that assassination would be the
only way to stop him. He would have to declare himself Oligarch soon and have them all rounded up.

The tall Captain stood there gasping for air, like a
beached fish. He was wearing a sleeveless chain mail
shirt covered with silver scales, and on his head rested
a blue-plumed helmet of the Blue Regiment. A golden
hue covered the skin around his nose and eyes reaching up to his forehead, while the rest of his face was
a milky white—except for the two dark brown stripes
which ran down from beneath each eye to join the
brown collar at his neck. His massive arms were

colored a light tan with offsetting dark brown diamonds splashed with gold in the center.

"What is this all about?"

"I'm sorry to disturb you, First Elder," panted Captain Sarel, "but the hatchery has been defiled."

"What!" gasped the Elder, rising from his throne to his feet. His bronze-colored face turned to copper and he almost dropped his staff of office. "What happened?"

"Someone has broken into the hatchery and taken the sacred eggs."

"By the Holy Serpent," croaked the First Elder, falling back down into his throne. "How many of them were taken?"

"It was a well-planned operation and they stole all but two or three. The hatchery guards were brutally murdered and all the attendants were poisoned."

"Did anyone get a look at these fiends?"

"Not anybody who is still alive. It's almost certain that they struck near the middle of the sleeping period."

"Has the news reached the city yet?"

"Yes, and it is spreading through Buzthara like a fire through a stand of trees."

The First Elder groaned. During the last few days, the city had been as active as a volcano waiting to erupt. Rumors, wild tales, and innuendos bubbling through the streets causing tempers to flair and loyalties to change. This wasn't the time for such news. The sacred eggs missing! The only thing he could think of that would have been worse, was if the cavern ceiling had started to collapse. "How is the city reacting?"

"As I made my way to the Council Hall," said Captain Sarel, "I saw a mob of clansmen racing down the street in search of humans responsible for this."

"Humans!"

"Apparently, they think that only humans would have been capable of such an atrocity. They are now seeking their vengeance in the city streets. I saw them stone one human they had found walking down the street. I even heard talk of the mob storming the human enclave and killing every human in Buzthara!"

The First Elder suddenly felt his spirits lift and he had to hold back a smile. It would fit right into his plans if the clansmen of Buzthara murdered the city's humans with their own hands. It would make it very difficult for them to complain, when he did the same all over Seker, until there wasn't a human left on the whole planet.

He needed to talk to his supporters, he decided; new plans had to be formulated. "Take as many guards as you think you'll need, Captain, and bring the High Priest of Set to my chambers."

"Yes, First Elder," returned the Captain, snapping to attention. "I shall return posthaste."

When the Captain left the Council Hall, he found the streets empty and ominously quiet. If it hadn't been for the occasional body lying lifeless in the street, he might have been able to convince himself that all was well. After walking three blocks he began to have trouble seeing, it was as though a dark blanket were being lowered down upon the city. He was starting to chide himself for being childish, when one of the guards mentioned having the same problem. Then he caught the acrid odor of smoke. Almost immediately, he began to have difficulty breathing as his heart began to beat against his chest. In the distance he could see long lines of smoke poking at the ceiling. He began to walk faster. There was nothing more dangerous in an underground city than fire. Didn't the fools know that, he thought to himself angrily. He sincerely hoped the city guard restored order soon; it wouldn't take too many fires to turn Buzthara into a smoke-filled death trap.

As he was pounding on the front door of the temple, he saw a squadron of mounted gardsmen tear through the plaza with their red cloaks streaming behind them. He watched as they raced down Council Way and wondered why, since he had just passed through that area and all had been quiet. His chain of thought was broken as the front door suddenly lurched open and several crossbows poked menacingly out of the opening.

After explaining his mission and showing the temple guards the snake's head ring given to him by the First Elder, he was led into the High Priest's audience room. As quickly as possible, he explained what had happened at the hatchery and told the Priest that the First Elder wanted to see him right away.

Over a half hour later, he and the High Priest left the Temple of Set with a dozen additional guards —most of them the famed Death Adders from the High Priest's own personal bodyguard. The black and grey striped Adders were members of the Elapidae Clan, the same clan as the High Priest, and were renowned for their loyalty and ferocity. The Death Adder's tribe, the Acanthophis Tribe, was very small and considered by the majority of genealogists to be an offshoot of the Naja Tribe. Its members served solely as guards for the Church of Set.

Temple Plaza and the nearby streets were deserted, but the howl of a large mob could be heard in the distance. The smoke was growing thicker and after coughing several times, the Captain led his party down Council Way toward the Council Hall. Less than two blocks away from the temple, the Captain heard moans of anguish coming from a motionless body near the front of a gutted shop.

As he started to walk towards the injured human, he heard the High Priest order, "Forget him, Captain, he's only a human."

"I don't care who he is," yelled the Captain over his shoulder. "He doesn't deserve to suffer needlessly."

"Captain!" screeched the High Priest. "I order you to ignore that wretch and to do your duty. It is most important that I see the First Elder right away."

So important, thought the Captain cynically, that you spent half an hour dawdling around the audience room. He reached the fallen human and turned him over. The man's face had been beaten until it was a bloody mess, and one arm was bent in several places where it wasn't supposed to bend. A cry of terrifying agony broke from the man's lips. The Captain had only heard its like once, and that's when he had been doing some hunting on the Tarsar Plain and he impaled a wild arixiath with a lance; its death-cry had been much the same.

"Captain," snarled the High Priest, "get away from that beast or I'll have you reported for dereliction of duty, and see to it personally that you are stripped of your rank."

The man's shirt was stained dark red and the Captain was forced to rip it so that he could see underneath. The chest cavity had collapsed, and he could see the porcelain white of the rib bones and the pink spongy tissue of the lungs. The sight sickened him and he had to steel himself for the task ahead. He didn't know why the man was still alive. Another scream pierced the air. He removed his kris from his belt and quickly drew the razor-sharp blade across the man's throat.

"I'm sorry that I misunderstood your intentions," said the High Priest, from behind. "The more of these vermin we destroy, the better."

The Captain rose to his feet and gave the High Priest a look of undisguised disgust.

The closer they came to Council Hall, the thicker the pungent smoke became. Soon the Captain found himself coughing almost constantly. The noise of the crowd was louder now, like the bellowing of a herd of tondars, and the Captain felt the worm of anxiety gnawing at his insides. Another squadron of cavalry raced down the narrow street, forcing them against the side.

People were beginning to crowd the street, and the Captain and his men had to force their way through the milling Ophidians. A thick haze made it very difficult to see, and he was forced to depend upon his heat receptors to lead his party through the growing mob. He ordered his men into a wedge-shaped formation after one of them was struck by a club, and they were forced to contest every meter of their passage. The mob was growing angrier and several times they had to use their spears to keep them back

Council Way ended at the foot of Balor Street where it faced the Council Hall building, a fifteen-meter high stone edifice. Balor Street itself was the scene of utter pandemonium. Fighting and screaming Ophidians of every color and description were rioting in a mad frenzy. Council Hall itself was their target and the Captain had to shake his head in disbelief. Many of the rioters were brandishing clubs, spears, swords, tools, and other improvised weapons. It was obvious that they were trying to gain entry to the towering building before them. Here and there mounted guardsmen were trying to subdue the angry crowd, but their efforts appeared futile. The Captain watched as one silver-helmeted guardsman was yanked off his arixiath and pulled down into the whirling vertex of the mob. He could see a large group of guardsmen valiantly guarding the Council Hall's great doors, and he decided that was where he would lead his party.

Maintaining their wedge-shaped formation, the Captain's party used their swords to hack a passage through the rioters. Undisciplined and untrained, the mob melted before the whirling blades. After several minutes they had worked their way to the Council doors, and Captain Sarel held a hasty conference with the commander of the guardsmen. Once he and the High Priest had convinced the harried commander of their identity, they were allowed entrance into the Council amid a loud roar by the maddened mob outside.

"What's going on out there," cried the First Elder, as the Captain and the High Priest stumbled into his chambers from the corridor outside.

"The rabble is storming Council Hall!" rasped the High Priest, who looked as though he were still shaken by the mob outside. His gold and scarlet robe was mussed and one sleeve was torn from where someone had tried, unsuccessfully, to yank him into the fury of the crowd.

The First Elder was about to snap back an angry retort when he noticed the dishevelled condition of his ally. "Does anybody *understand* what is happening out there?" he asked rhetorically. "First, I'm receiving reports that the populace is out hunting humans and planning to destroy Stinktown. The next thing I know is that they're trying to break into the Council Hall. What is this all about?"

"I think you had better call out the troops," advised the High Priest, his voice cracking several times. "We have the loyalty of the Blue Regiment, the Ragoor Swords, and possibly that of the Habor Guard. They've gone crazy out there and they must be stopped."

"If this rioting doesn't stop soon," said the First Elder, "I will call out the Bushmaster Brigade and have them deal with this insurrection."

"Who are they?"

The First Elder looked at the Captain suspiciously for a moment and then said, "I don't see any reason to keep their existence a secret any longer. They are a new body of Cerastes soldiers armed with weapons given to me by the off-worlders."

"You wouldn't use off-worlder weapons against an unarmed crowd?" the Captain asked in shock.

"Captain, they are attacking the Council Hall," cried the First Elder. "If necessary, I will do anything within my power to restore order to this city. Do I make myself clear? Now, find someone who knows what is going on out there."

This is madness, thought Captain Sarel to himself. He will destroy the city if he has his way.

A loud banging on the door brought all conversation to a halt. "Who is it?" shouted the First Elder, all ceremony and ritual forgotten in the heat of crisis.

"Counsellor Donal," answered an urgent voice. The Elder gave a nod and the emerald Pythoninae walked over and opened the door.

The Counsellor's toga was torn and ripped, and there was a jagged cut over one eye. "You'd better do something," he squeaked. "I almost didn't make it through the crowd." He shuddered and then added,

"They've gone crazy out there. Counsellor Jaforn stumbled and before the guard could help him to his feet, someone in the crowd had taken hold of him and he was gone." He gave a horrified gasp. "By the Great Serpent, they tore him into pieces. His arm landed right in front of me!"

"Calm down!" ordered the First Elder.

The Counsellor took several deep breaths and then stood still.

"Now, do *you* know what this is all about?"

"Yes," panted Counsellor Donal. "The people blame you for the violation of the hatchery. I know it is complete nonsense, but they believe it. They are no longer Ophidians, but," he spat in disgust, *"humans."*

"What!" roared the First Elder. "Who is responsible for these lies? It must be the humans and their allies, the Magi. But why would they suddenly turn on me, when earlier they were convinced that it was the humans who had committed this sacrilege."

"I don't know," cringed the Counsellor. "But it is being said that you have become mad."

"Mad!"

"Yes," added the Counsellor hastily. "It is running through the streets that your lust for power has driven you into insanity. Not that there is any truth to such babble, of course, First Elder."

"Counsellor, I want you to have Colonel Zant brought here to my chambers. It is time that I unleashed the Bushmaster Brigade. *Mad!* Why, I'll teach them!"

Thirteen

WATCHING THE CONSTANT stream of Ophidians and humans coming in and out of the room, Veblen found it almost hard to believe that this was the peaceful center of learning that he first entered a week ago. The university's Regent's Room was now the command headquarters for the Covenant forces; the name given to all those who opposed the First Elder and his allies. Tension and energy filled the air like static electricity and Veblen felt, for the first time since he had landed on Seker, that events were beginning to come to a head.

He would have been enjoying himself if it hadn't been for the anxiety he felt over Vera's safety. He had spent several days searching for her, but had been forced to give up when the investigation failed to turn up any clues. Vera's captors had been quick and thorough, and had left nothing for him to follow up. It had been a difficult decision to make, but they had needed him at the university, and he knew deep inside that there was little he could do for Vera until he had more information. It was his guess that Vera had either been abducted by the First Elder's henchmen or by the off-worlders, and that she would be discovered when they were defeated. If they *were* defeated! And if she were still alive? Every day he was realizing more and more just how much he missed Vera, with her sharp wit and deep brown eyes. Somehow, he had allowed himself to feel more for her than he had felt for any other person in a long, long time. He still wasn't sure how it had happened.

A messenger from the communication room—where most of the high-frequency transmission equipment brought by Veblen, and that used by the local Informants, was being used for surveillance purposes—hurried over to where Veblen and the Master Magus were sitting. "The First Elder's army has started to attack."

"Where?" asked Veblen.

"Down by the docks."

"Well," said the Master Magus, "it has finally started. I only wish we were better prepared."

"I'm surprised he gave us this much time," answered Veblen. "I had fully expected him to take over the city right after the Council Hall massacre."

Another messenger rushed up to them, saying, "The First Elder has just declared himself Oligarch. It is all over the city, Master."

The Master Magus turned towards Veblen. "It appears that today is the day." Then he looked at the messenger and ordered, "Find Marshal Sarel and have him report to me at once."

Several minutes later, Marshal Sarel, formerly Captain Sarel of the Blue Regiment, walked into the Regent's Room. He had been one of the first to leave the First Elder's ranks right after the Council Hall massacre. Over the protests of his commander, General Gallon, he had defected with about half of the Blue Regiment. As the highest ranking Covenant officer, he had been given command over the Covenant's forces, consisting of eight companies from the Blue Regiment, a surface command called the Buzthara Cavalry, a regiment bound to the Bitis Tribe called the Blood Pythons—and a number of companies that had formely served with the city guard and the harbor guard. These soldiers, along with ten thousand Ophidian and human volunteers, made up the bulk of the Marshal's command, which gave the Covenant a force about one-half the size of that fielded by the new Oligarch.

"You've heard the news," said the Master Magus as the Marshal approached.

"Yes," answered Marshal Sarel. "I've been expecting them to attack the waterfront for days."

"Why the waterfront?" asked Veblen.

"Whoever holds the docks of Buzthara, controls the city. Not only do most of the city's supplies come in by barge, but so will the reinforcements from the outlying cities. When the First Elder had his troops use off-worlder weapons to drive away the crowd outside of the Council Hall, he committed an atrocity that alienated him from everyone but his closest supporters. He has lost most of his support outside of the city, and I'm sure that he realizes that he must defeat our forces before the outlying cities have time to send their soldiers to our aid. Because once the First Elder rules Buzthara, he will rule Seker."

"How long will our forces be able to hold the waterfront?"

"No more than three or four days," answered the Marshal, "and that's only because the Oligarch's men will have to take each building one at a time.

We wouldn't stand a chance out in the open, not with our untrained forces against the off-worlder's weapons."

"When will the first reinforcements begin to arrive?"

"It will be days, and then not enough to make any difference right away."

"If the Oligarch's forces take over the waterfront, how long will we be able to hold the city then?" asked Veblen, racking his brain for some kind of solution to their dilemma. He knew that if the city fell there would be almost no way in which he could complete his mission. In that case, Vera might be lost forever. . . .

"I'm sure we could hold the city for at least a week," said Marshal Sarel. "Most of Buzthara's food comes from the surface, and there are wells throughout the city to draw fresh water from. However, the Oligarch will have the military advantage, and while we have the people's support, I don't know how long that will last when matched against the bullets of the Oligarch's army."

"The 'gifted' have told all of Seker about our plight," said the Master Magus, "but it appears that if we can't hold the city, they will be unable to help. Our situation looks dismal. What will we do, Marshal, if we are forced to abandon Buzthara?"

"We will evacuate the city, which means that there is only one place we can go. The surface."

"The surface!" cried the Master Magus. "But the hardships on the women and the young. . . . We would have to leave the hatchery . . . and the university . . . and the books. . . ."

"Yes," said the Marshal, "and we will be at the mercy of the Thadrons. I'm glad that it is our side that believes in human rights . . . I only hope that up there they know it too."

"If we're forced to evacuate," said the Master, "we will have to take every human in the city with us. Otherwise, they will all be murdered in the Oligarch's pogrom."

"Maybe they'll be able to help us survive up there," said the Marshal, with a faint smile. "Though I don't know what for."

"The surface," repeated Veblen, his voice distant, "I think I may have the answer."

"Answer to what?"

"I don't want to raise any false hopes, so I'll tell you about it after I check with Jarl."

"Yes, Proctor," whined Brother Bernard, "and I brought the female Investigator along with me."

A female Investigator, thought the Proctor with contempt. As far as he was concerned women had no use outside of their necessary function in the breeder colonies, and they wouldn't even be needed there except that the fetal tanks continually showed an inexplicably high infant-mortality rate. There had never been a woman aboard *The Sword of Wrath* before, but he should have thought about that when he gave his orders. His thoughts were beginning to stir and he suddenly realized that his mind was no longer the serene pool that it had been before his disruptive contact with Brother Bernard. "I thought your instructions were to bring both of the Investigators to the ship."

"I am aware of my failure," said the Brother, cringing. "But the Investigator spent most of his time inside the university and there was no way I could reach him."

"Didn't he try to find his assistant?"

"Yes . . . but, Proctor, he was guarded well. I was afraid to cause a scene. If I would have been captured, there would have been no way for you to rescue me," he finished, with a shudder.

The Proctor gave the Brother a look of total disdain and instantly realized, with a shock that jolted him, that he hated the incompetent wretch. There was no way he would be able to tolerate the presence of such an emotional carrier all the way back to Capek: He would have to make sure Brother Bernard never left Seker. The Brother was a one-man emotional epidemic and was a danger to everyone he came in contact with. "I order you to return to Buzthara until the Anomian Investigator is captured."

"But . . . ," sputtered Brother Bernard, "our mission has been successfully completed and we have recovered enough radioactive ore to leave this horrible place. Why do you want to send me back down there?"

He deserves this, thought the Proctor to himself, as he repressed a grin. "It will be another four to five days before all the ore has been refined, and you have until then to locate and take the Investigator."

"But why do we need him," wailed the Brother. "We've concluded Operation Psi and we're almost ready to leave!"

"Because it is possible that the Investigator may find some way to foul our plans."

"But that's not possible!" cried the Brother in a voice verging on panic. "Even if he had an available ship, it would be no match for a battle cruiser like *The Sword of Wrath*, or our sensors would have located her long ago."

He doesn't even have any pride left, thought the

Proctor contemptuously. It was fortunate that he would not have to suffer his presence for long. "Look," he continued, in a no-nonsense tone of voice, "your orders are to return to Seker and capture the Investigator. If you are not successful, as far as I'm concerned, you can stay there until you rot."

The Brother's face turned white with fear and he began to plead. "But you don't understand, Proctor, I can't stand being around those snake-men any longer. . . ." His whole body began to shake and his voice grew louder. "There's a war going on down there too—I might be killed." He fell down on his knees. "Please, I beg you. . . ."

The Proctor was no longer enjoying the Brother's performance; it was beginning to make him ill. Never before in over two thousand years of life had he ever seen a member of the Brotherhood so tainted with the curse of emotions. Death for such a pariah could only be seen as a blessing. Turning to the Guardian, who stood at the side of his desk, he commanded, "Guardian, take this man and see that he is placed aboard the shuttle and sent back to Seker immediately. Put him in one of the specimen holds. It would not be good for morale if the crew were to see such sickness in one who wears the purple of the Brotherhood."

The giant Guardian walked over to the now prostrate Brother and lifted him up to his feet, and then guided him out of the Proctor's cabin.

Fourteen

BY THE TIME THE THADRON war camp had come into sight, Veblen was almost in too much pain to care. Three hours on the back of a galloping arixiath had left him sore and hurting in places he didn't like to mention in mixed company. While the riding arixiaths were a much smaller bred than those used to pull the canal barges, they were still intended for someone much larger than he was, like one of the tall Boidae guardsmen. It was Veblen's first ride on an animal and hopefully his last. He had been so busy just trying to keep on the arixiath's broad back that he hadn't even been able to enjoy the lush vegetation and the alien landscape. Even the fresh air and sunshine seemed to pall because of the aches and pains.

The nomad's tents littered the plain like toadstools in a forest clearing, and Veblen momentarily took his mind off his discomforts to review his operation. It had been his idea to contact the surface tribes and form an alliance with them against the Oligarch. Without outside help, it was obvious that the outnumbered and underarmed Covenant forces would soon have to yield the city to the Oligarch's army. The enemy forces already held a strong position along the waterfront, and only the last-minute arrival of reinforcements from the nearby cities of Nueria and Lattur had stopped a complete rout along the docks. More trained troops were needed desperately by the Covenant to make up for the Oligarch's advantage in trained soldiers and advanced weaponry.

Veblen and Jarl had left the besieged city for the surface where they contacted the humans who lived in the compounds provided by their Ophidian overlords. His theory had been that there was more intercourse between the enslaved humans and the nomad tribes than the Ophidians were aware of. Veblen had decided to visit the humans who lived and worked in the surface compounds, and see if they would help him contact the Thadrons. After all, the Oligarch's feelings toward Seker's humans were well known, and it was obvious to Veblen that the only way the human population on Seker was going to avoid a horrible blood bath was to join forces with the Covenant. Whether the surface humans, and the Thadrons, saw it that way was the critical issue.

Alone, Veblen had entered one of the major compounds to talk to their representatives. He had stated his case and reminded them of the need for speed. After he had finished, Elder Orthon, one of their leaders, had verified his information and agreed that an alliance would be to everyone's advantage. He had then told Veblen he would arrange a meeting with Sontar Varn, the Thadron warlord, and use his influence to gain support for the alliance. According to the Elder—after the hatchery incident and the Council Hall massacre—the city and surface humans had reached the conclusion that should the First Elder take control of Buzthara, which it had certainly looked like he was able to do, then they would all soon be in great danger. This information had then been quickly relayed to the Thadrons, the only humans on Seker capable of organized armed resistance. In response, the surface nomads had called a war council, and decided to send out a summons to all the Thadrons on the continent to join an interclan war party. Since that time, Thadrons—by the hundreds and thousands—had been arriving daily at the nomad encampment and were now debating on whether to wait for the Ophidians to come to them, or whether to enter the air ducts and besiege Buzthara.

Seeing a group of Thadrons mounted on miniature arixiaths coming out to meet them, Veblen wasn't sure whether he should feel envious over their smaller mounts, or relieved that the journey was finally coming to an end. He and his four companions, Jarl Sorgent, the Elder Orthon and two others from the compound, halted their arixiaths, and then the Elder conferred with the solemn Thadrons.

They were led to a large tent and told to wait for a summons from Sontar. The tent was made out of tanned hides and there were fur-covered pillows for their seating comfort. Veblen looked at them longingly, but the saddle sores along the inside and back of his legs made it too painful to sit unless absolutely necessary.

After an hour's wait, they were escorted by two stone-faced warriors into the warlord's tent. Sontar Varn was not the bear-of-a-man nomad leader that Veblen had expected to see. While his face and hands were weathered and leathery, his features were well formed and slightly effeminate; however there was nothing womanly about his coal black eyes, and the cruel twist of his thin lips. A thick fur cloak hid most of his body, but Veblen knew there was corded muscle in those arms when he shook the warlord's hand in greeting.

"Why have you brought these strangers to my camp, Elder," asked Sontar, in a voice that boomed like a distant cannon shot, and gave Veblen another clue to the source of the warlord's charisma.

"Warlord, this man here," he said, pointing to Veblen, "claims to be an emissary from those inside Buzthara who would like to help us stop the Oligarch from taking over the city."

Sontar gave Veblen a careful examination and then asked, "Why have you come to me for help?"

Veblen knew that he was under close scrutiny and decided that his wisest move would be to give the whole truth. "I represent a coalition of humans and Ophidians called the Covenant. It is our desire to stop the Oligarch before he takes power and destroys Buzthara and all the humans on Seker. . . ."

"No!" roared the warlord. "That will never happen! We will chase the snake-people down deep into the earth where they belong. They will never stop us. We have waited a long time to take our revenge, but now the time has come."

A cheer went up from the assembled war chieftains and several of the guards anxiously stuck their heads into the tent to see what all the commotion was about.

"Warlord," said Veblen as soon as the cheering had stopped, "not all of the Ophidians are against the humans." Veblen was interrupted by several derogatory shouts and paused until the tent had quieted again. "These Ophidians are members of the Covenant and are as interested in human liberation as Ophidian liberation. They need your help to defeat the Oligarch and his army. If they lose their battle, then all Seker has lost and all that live on it will bow before the blades of the Oligarch."

"Not when he meets us," shouted the warlord, who threw his knife into the ground in front of Veblen. "Never in our history has such an army been brought together." His arms circumscribed all the area around him, and then he added, "Over one hundred clans ride under the sign of the Drota. We shall smoke the snake-people out of their burrows and destroy them for all time."

There was more cheering and shouting.

The warlord continued, "The fattened tondar was sacrificed and the augors claimed that we shall be triumphant over the snake-people. We will kill them all."

Elder Orthon gave Veblen a look of despair. Veblen had figured that he might take some doing to convince them that it was in their best interest to ally themselves with the Covenant; but he had not expected to run into a ferrocene wall of resistance. "Look," exclaimed Veblen, "you will be fighting against more than just the Ophidians. The Oligarch's men are armed with off-world weapons which can fire from horizon to horizon."

Several of the chieftains began to whisper to each other.

Sontar silenced the lesser chieftains with a freezing glare and then declared; "Their weapons may be mighty, but our hearts are filled with courage and we shall overcome them."

The fate of Seker, Vera's life, and the success of his mission all depended upon the outcome of this meeting; therefore, Veblen felt justified in making a desperate move.

His eyes found a suitable target and his hand darted inside his shirt, drew his laser out, flicked it to full power, aimed it, and fired it. The saddle glared for a moment and then disappeared in a ball of flame. Smoke filled the room and Veblen felt his arms being grabbed from behind. A couple of the chieftains drew their swords while others ran towards Veblen.

Veblen was roughly brought before the warlord, whose face was livid with anger.

"Stake him out," one chieftain cried.

Sontar held his hands out for silence, looking at Veblen, and demanded, "What was the meaning of this?"

Veblen looked him right in the eye. "Since you were not listening to me, I felt it necessary to offer proof of my claims."

The veins on Sontar's forehead did a little dance and Veblen hoped that the warlord was as uninformed about the off-worlder weapons as he had assumed.

"Continue," ordered the warlord through tightened lips.

Veblen paused a moment to restore his calm. "This weapon I have shown you is but one small gun, and yet you all saw the destruction it was able to cause."

A number of the chieftains nodded their agreement.

"The Oligarch's men have many such weapons and they will use them to destroy you all. Only if you are allied with the Covenant forces will there be enough men to stop the Oligarch. It is for you and the Ophidians, that I ask you to give serious thought to what I have said before this council."

136

An old chieftain, bent and withered with age, spoke up. "Warlord, I ask you to give consideration to what this city dweller has said. If he has lied to us, I'm sure that we will be able to give justice to the snake-people and his allies once the Oligarch has been destroyed. I say that we join forces with this Covenant and help bring down the Oligarch."

The majority of the chieftains voiced their agreement and the warlord gave Veblen a look of dark hostility. "Bring the sun gun to me," he ordered, and then gave the machined piece of metal careful scrutiny. Looking up, he told the guards, "Remove the city dwellers." To the assembled chieftains he said, "We shall discuss the city dweller's words and see if there is any merit to his proposal."

Fifteen

"I WOULDN'T BELIEVE IT, except that it's happening right in front of my eyes," cried Marshal Sarel as the wave of Ophidian and human soldiers charged over the broken wreckage of what once had been a stone warehouse. A few scattered shots still rang out, but the once invincible Bushmaster brigade had been broken and many of the shots were coming from confiscated weapons. A few survivors tried to escape from the ruins, but they were quickly rounded up.

Veblen heard the crack of a catapult and watched as the grey boulder crashed into a broken wall. The introduction of catapults by Veblen, while a violation of the Protectorate's law of cultural noninterference, had—along with the Thadron warriors—allowed the Covenant's forces to turn what had looked like inevitable defeat three days before, into a successful victory over the Oligarch's main force.

"We're not finished yet," said Veblen to the Marshal, as he examined the jagged ruins and still forms that littered the waterfront. Many of the bodies were human, both city dweller and surface nomad, and Veblen made a promise to himself to see that their sacrifice had not been made in vain. He owed them that much, at least; it had been the humans who had comprised the majority of the suicidal waves which had beaten against the enemy time after time, until his defenses had broken. The waterfront was now in smoldering ruins and thousands of corpses clogged the streets. Smoke permeated the air and Veblen found it difficult to breathe even with his improvised gas mask on; he fully sympathized with those who were fighting and running in the murky air.

He saw the distant flash of a laser. He was surprised that it still had any charge left and decided that Sontar must be using it with care. The laser had been the price for the warlord's support: a way for him to save face. Sontar had not been pleased when the council of chieftains had voted against him and decided to join forces with the Covenant. Veblen had felt that the laser had been a small price to pay for his appeasement.

The last of the Oligarch's soldiers began their retreat and the Covenant's forces started to run after the fleeing Ophidians, brandishing their weapons.

"Well, we're finished here," Marshal Sorel said.

"Now we only have one last nut to crack," said Veblen wearily.

"I'm sure that we'll find her there," said the Marshal with a reassuring smile.

Veblen looked at the Ophidian in surprise and then gave him a tired smile. As closely as they had worked the past three days, it was no wonder that the Marshal knew what was troubling his mind. During the last two sleeping periods, when there had been a lull in fighting long enough to allow him a couple hours of sleep, he had awakened in the midst of a horrifying nightmare.

Each time he had been examining an abandoned ruin when he had suddenly come upon Vera's body, limp and lifeless. Now every time an enemy position was overrun he would wait pensively, expecting Vera's body to turn up among the dead defenders. But now there was only one place left where she could be, Council Hall. That is, if she was still on Seker and if not. . . . He was too tired and too weary to continue that train of thought. "How long will the siege take?" he asked.

"Not long," replied the Marshal cheerfully. "Those catapults of yours will bring Council Hall tumbling right down around them. While the Council Hall might be quite an obstacle to an unarmed crowd, we'll make short work of it."

"All my plans have come to naught," cried the Oligarch, as the walls of his inner sanctum shuddered again. One of the tapers fell from its holder on the wall in a cascade of sparks and the Oligarch's Pythoninae bodyguard ran over and returned it to its proper place.

"And it's all your fault," he added, rising to his feet and then kicking the purple-robed prisoner who lay before his throne. "Where is the aid you promised me, off-worlder?"

The Brother made an incoherent wail and the Oligarch kicked him again.

Everything had suddenly gone all wrong, thought the Oligarch to himself bitterly, and it had all started when the hatchery had been violated—and he had been falsely accused of the crime. Then there had been the Council Hall massacre, where his newly armed brigade had gleefully butchered the mob outside. Their over-zealous reaction had cost him the support of the city. Yet, he still might have gained control over Buzthara, if it hadn't been for the timely arrival of the surface dwellers. It had been the human factor that had brought about his defeat: an intangible in his plans of conquest. Those vile vegetable eaters were the instrument of his downfall. It was almost more than his old heart could bear, and it began to make an angry drum beat against his chest. He slumped back down into his thone, sucked in air, and glared at the miserable wretch at his feet.

"Untie him," he ordered his bodyguard, pointing to the man bound at his feet. After taking several deep breaths, he demanded, "Contact your ship, off-worlder, and tell them to give me the help you promised."

The plump Brother remained lying on the floor rubbing his bruised wrists.

"If you value your life, answer me, animal," cried the Oligarch, clutching his chest.

The Brother wobbled to his feet and then began to beseech the Oligarch. "My communicator is broken and I can no longer contact the ship. But even if I could, they would not help you. The ship's weapons are useless here. We're all doomed!"

"Liar!" screamed the Oligarch, trying unsuccessfully to come to his feet.

The door crashed open and General Gallon, his magnificent uniform in tatters, ran into the chamber followed by several other officers.

"What's wrong?"

"The enemy has broken down the gates. . . ."

"Already!" His face became a strange hue.

"Yes, Oligarch. They were using machines to cast boulders at the Council building and the whole front wall caved in. The destruction was beyond belief, and then they swarmed in like a wild heard of arixiaths. We just barely managed to escape. . . ."

"Then they're on their way," interrupted the Oligarch, realizing with a jolt that there wasn't going to be any last-minute miracle to save his throne.

"Any minute now," answered the General.

The room shook again violently, throwing the Oligarch against the hard stone floor.

"Are you all right?"

The Oligarch pulled himself upright, blood dribbling from the corner of his mouth and down his chin. "I'm still alive," he answered. "Is there a chance we can fight our way out?"

"I'm afraid it is too late now," answered General Gallon.

Reaching down to his belt, the Oligarch pulled a wickedly curved dagger from its scabbard, lunged forward, drew his arm back, and buried it to its hilt in the Brother's purple robe. The Brother fell to the floor on his back and a dark black stain began to dampen the front of his habit.

That was one human he would see in Cthor's realm, thought the Oligarch, falling to the floor as his overtaxed heart failed from the strain he had placed on it. The cool waters of death washed the bitterness of defeat from his mind and his body made one final convulsion before it came to a final rest.

"There he is," said the blue-plumed officer, pointing to the sprawling form of the dead Oligarch, his face twisted into a macabre mask.

The Marshal picked up the limp hand and felt for a pulse just to make sure. Nodding his head in agreement, he swore, "The old bugger's heart must have given out. Damn it, I would have liked to have seen him die the hard way."

Veblen missed most of the Marshal's statement; he was too busy staring in disbelief at the purple-robed body with the gilded knife handle sticking out. So it was the Brotherhood which was behind all the mischief on Seker, he thought to himself, as he fell down on his knees. An agonizing groan from the Brother gave his hopes wings. Leaning over the Brother's face, he removed the cowl and studied his round-faced adversary. He checked the pulse and found it weak but steady. Maybe the Brother's wound wasn't fatal? However, he decided not to remove the dagger himself and asked the Marshal to call for a surgeon.

The Brother must have heard his voice for his mouth fell open and he moaned. Veblen took heart until he saw a small stream of blood run out his mouth. "Can you talk?" he asked.

"I think so," groaned the Brother.

"I've sent for a doctor and he will be here in a couple of minutes," said Veblen.

The Brother nodded.

"Do you think you can answer a few questions?"

After coughing up a clot of black blood, he whispered, "I'd do anything to pay back that metal-hearted monster for abandoning me on this ghastly planet."

"What does the Brotherhood want with Seker?"

"It is the abilities of the 'gifted' that the Prime Monitor is interested in . . . ," he coughed several time and then continued. "I was the one who had the sacred eggs stolen from the hatchery." He made a high-pitched giggle and then added, "It's almost fun-

143

ny how it all backfired and ruined our plans."

"Go on," encouraged Veblen. "What does the Prime Monitor want with the sacred eggs?"

"The Prime Monitor wants to study them so he can learn what part of the mind is responsible for their psychic abilities." The Brother paused briefly to take several wheezing breaths, and Veblen noticed that his globular cheeks were covered with tiny wet beads. "When this is determined, the Prime Monitor will use this information to have genetic alterations made on selected subjects in the breeder colonies. Once these experiments have come to a successful conclusion, he will use these psychics to extend his control throughout the galaxies of man and beyond."

Veblen felt as though a cold rod had been inserted in his spine. "How many ships do you have?"

The Brother started to choke and gasp, and for a second, Veblen thought he was finished. His body shuddered twice and then he continued. "One ship, Investigator, a full-strength battle cruiser. We had three supporting craft, but they were destroyed coming through the blockade."

Veblen quickly tried to sort out the questions in his mind so that he only asked the most important. He wasn't sure that the Brother would live much longer. "Why did you set up a base in the Royd Mountains?"

"Reaction drive damaged during battle . . . forced to jettison most of our radioactive fuel. We were mining more fuel so that we could leave. . . ."

Suddenly Veblen realized that he hadn't asked about Vera. "What about my assistant, Vera Holleran? Do you know what happened to her?" He watched the Brother's labored breathing. "Answer me." he shouted, as the Brother began to shake and a bright red foam appeared on his lips. He had to stop himself from grasping the Brother and wringing the last few words from him mouth.

"She's aboard *The Sword of Wrath*," gasped the dying Brother. "She was still alive when I saw her last but. . . .'"

Veblen took hold of the Brother by the shoulders, but it was too late.

"Here's the surgeon," announced the Marshal.

"Never mind," said Veblen. "He's not going to say anything more."

"Did you learn anything?"

"Yes," mumbled Veblen, more to himself than to anyone else. "But not near enough, I'm afraid."

Sixteen

How could Vera be rescued, Veblen asked himself over and over. The Brotherhood's ship would be leaving any day now to return to the Esoterics. Once it had left, Vera would be beyond his help or anyone else's. What her eventual fate might me, he was afraid to guess. Once they had removed every piece of useful information from her brain, they would probably put her coldly to death, if she was lucky. There was no place in the Esoterics for a woman of Vera's intelligence and independence; she was no docile cow to be pastured out in one of the breeder colonies.

"Why so glum?" asked the Master Magus, setting down a stack of reports on the city's damage that he had just been reading. "We may have lost the sacred eggs but they are replaceable."

"I was just thinking about Vera," Veblen said. "I have to come up with some way to save her, but I can't think of a single idea."

"You really do care for her," said the Master Magus weaving his head back and forth sympathetically. "If there is anything we can do, don't hesitate to ask. For we will never be able to repay you for all you have done to help Seker."

"I appreciate your offer, but without an armed spaceship, I don't know what I can do."

"I know of something we can try," said the Master Magus. Motioning to one of the students, who was dressed in a white tunic, he said, "Find the Magus Kirl and tell him that I want to see him."

"What's your idea?" asked Veblen, as they waited for the Magus to arrive.

"I want Kirl to bring one of the 'gifted' before us. One who is capable of mindspeak. With his help we may be able to contact Vera and you will be able to find out how she is doing."

"Can the 'gifted' speak thoughts over that great a distance?"

"Certainly," the Master Magus answered. "It is far easier for one of the 'gifted' to mindspeak or mindlisten over a long distance, where there are few minds, than for him to try and establish contact within Buzthara where there are many minds to create interference."

"So that is why you didn't use the 'gifted' to monitor the Oligarch and his counsellors?"

"Yes, although there were several other important ramifications that had to be taken into account. It is against our law to mindlisten without the other's permission in advance. We gave this issue serious consideration and arrived at the conclusion that it does not make any more sense for an engineer to undermine a road that he is building, than it does for a political leader to break the laws he is trying to save. This is what brought about the Oligarch's downfall. We Ophidians set great store in our laws and traditions, which may be why our government has retained its stability for so long."

"I can see that there is a great deal we humans can learn from your people."

Magus Kirl appeared several minutes later, listened to the Master's instructions, and returned shortly with a slim Ophidian marked by even bands of black and white.

Outside of the small ridge that began at the front of his head and ended where the skull joined the spine, the 'gifted' Ophidian was similar to every other one that Veblen had seen. Veblen gave the Ophidian telepath a brief description of Vera, and then he assumed the full lotus position and went into a trance state.

"One day," whispered the Master Magus to Veblen, as they watched the motionless telepath, "mind-listen will be as easy for them as talking is now. We have bred the 'gifted' lines for millenniums to get this far, and I'm sure that it will take even longer for these traits to breed true, but someday all of us will have these abilities."

The Ophidian telepath suddenly opened his eyes and began to speak, "Vera is fine," said the telepath in a dull monotone. "She has been kept prisoner in a cabin by herself and she has not been harmed."

"That's something to be thankful for," said Veblen. "Ask her if there is anything we do to help her?"

The telepath paused for a moment and then began to speak, "She says that her captors are members of the Brotherhood and that the reason they came to Seker was to steal some of the 'gifted.' They will be leaving soon and she wants you to know that she has come to terms with her fate. She says that there are many things that she has left unfinished and unsaid, but is glad for one last chance to resolve some of them. Her last words are that she loves you and only wishes that she had made some meaningful demonstration of her affection while she had the chance."

Veblen felt as though someone had taken red-hot metal tongs and squeezed his heart with them. "Tell her that I love her too," he cried, "and that I won't rest until I find someway to rescue her."

The Master Magus looked at him sadly. "Too often the heart is at the mercy of the hands of fate."

The telepath was now out of his trance and was staring vacantly at the wall on the other side of the room.

Veblen felt like a man who had just learned from his doctor that he only had six more months to live. For the first time in his life he was in love, and he might never see her again. There had to be something he could do.

A student walked into the room, stood before the Master Magus, and said, "Master, the off-worlders have abandoned their base near Zendo."

"Are you sure?"

"Yes, Master. They took everything of value and destroyed what was left."

"Then they're gone," said Veblen sorrowfully. "That means they have the radioactive fuel they need to power their reaction drive."

"Then they'll be leaving our atmosphere soon?"

"Yes, which means that if we are going to stop them it has to be soon—before they leave their present orbit."

"What happened when you contacted your superiors?"

"They said there weren't any Anomian battle cruisers close enough to do us any good. So it is up to us." Veblen paused for over a minute and then said excitedly, "There may be a way we can stop them!"

"What is it?"

"Do any of the 'gifted' have the ability of psychokinesis? That is, the capability of moving fixed objects through concentration?"

"Yes, but I'm afraid that their mindcontrol is very limited. Our greatest successes have been with mindspeaking."

"Would it be possible for me to see a demonstration of their abilities?"

"Of course," said the Master Magus rising to his feet.

Another twelve hours and we will be on our way to Capek, thought the Proctor, as he waited for the woman prisoner to be brought into his cabin. But best of all, he was rid of Brother Bernard for good. It had been over thirty hours since he had last heard from him, when the Brother had called begging to allow him to return to the ship. He had claimed that the Oligarch's forces were on the verge of defeat. He had refused, of course, since the Oligarch's reverses were not his concern, and Brother Bernard had not completed his mission on time. It would be nice, he thought, if the poor imbecile was still alive. Who could guess what horrible tortures the Ophidian's mind might devise for the Brother's amusement.

He listened to himself chuckle and then stopped in sudden horror. His prolonged exposure to that vile creature had him reacting like a lay. The next month or two would have to be spent in complete isolation while he practiced the cleansing exercises and purged the emotional infection out of his system. He only hoped that he hadn't been permanently corrupted by his association with that animal. How he longed for the bliss of objectivity and emotional disassociation.

The Heraldkey began its song and he activated the door mechanism. In walked the Guardian with the female prisoner, her eyes wide with fear. "What do you want with me?" she asked, a slight quiver betraying her fear.

"Just a preliminary session with the mind-probe," he answered, while clinically observing her reaction. He saw her flinch but otherwise she maintained her emotional control. He nodded his head in approval. This was going to be an interesting session, he thought, as he ordered the Guardian to seat her at the encephalomonitor.

After one capsule of releasophine, she would tell him everything he wanted to know; while the encephalomonitor kept track of all the emotions and impressions that were stirred up by his questioning. Just as he was about to order the Guardian to give her the releasophine, he heard the buzz of the ship's communicator.

He pressed the receive button and saw the worried face of Captain Jenen appear on the screen. "What is it?" he asked.

"Sorry to disturb you, Proctor, but we have run into an unprecedented problem with the reaction drive. The reaction mass is dead. There aren't any radioactive particles being emitted. It's the damndest thing I've ever seen. . . ."

"Are you positive that what you took off Seker was uranium, or was it just dirt?" interrupted the Proctor sarcastically.

"It was uranium," stated the Chief Engineer, whose

face appeared next to that of the Captain's. "I'd stake my career on it."

"You already have," returned the Proctor.

The Chief Engineer blanched, but continued. "Up until five minutes ago, it was a normal atomic pile. But something is inhibiting it. I even pulled all the dampening rods and it didn't make any difference. It's contrary to the laws of physics. Maybe you had better come down here, Proctor, and see for yourself."

Seventeen

"How are the 'gifted' holding up?" asked the Master Magus, as Veblen walked into the Regent's Room.

"Not too well," Veblen said. "One of the weaker ones dropped from exhaustion and we had to make a substitution with a young girl."

"How important is it to have six minds in the mental matrix?"

"I'd like to have more than six," answered Veblen, "but with as few adepts as we have at mindcontrol, that was the optimum number. With any less, I'm not sure we would be able to control the reaction mass of the Proctor's ship."

"Then how much longer do you think they will be able to maintain their control?"

"A couple of hours, at most," said Veblen, as he eased himself into the seat next to the Master Magus. His body was almost numb with fatigue and he had to shake himself to keep alert. To many crises and sleepless nights had taken their toll. "Though I must admit," he added, "that they have already more than exceeded my expectations. I'm sure that by now the Captain of the Brotherhood's ship is going into paroxysms of rage."

The Ophidian smiled. "Don't you think we had better make contact with their ship before too long?"

"Yes, I agree," said Veblen hesitantly; he was well aware of exactly how much counted upon the success of their stratagem. "I wouldn't want to cut it too close, even though they have no idea of how long we can hold their ship in its present orbit. Hopefully, they will be anxious to bargain."

Veblen activated the high frequency transmitter—which had formerly been used for transmissions between Informants and Anomian survey craft—and began to tune in different frequencies. About a minute later he made contact with *The Sword of Wrath's* communications officer and he asked to speak to whoever was in command.

The Proctor's voice immediately sounded through the room, "Who is it?"

"Investigator Thorstein Veblen, of the Anomian Bureau of Extraterrestrial Investigations."

"I take it that you're the one who is responsible for the loss of our reaction mass. I order you to desist at once or face grave consequences."

"Who am I speaking to?" asked Veblen.

"I am Proctor Z-412-00F432CR," answered a cold mechanical voice. "Now I am warning you, release my ship or else."

"I will release the control we have established over the fissionable fuel of your ship's reaction drive, when you have released my assistant Investigator and the twelve eggs which were forcibly removed from the hatchery."

"I will agree to return your assistant, but the eggs

are in my care and there they will remain."

"Then no deal," said Veblen harshly. "We shall hold you in your present position until next week when the Anomian battle cruiser, the *Inxtal*, arrives." While Veblen had made an emergency Tachyon beam call to Anomia, they had told him there were no ships in the immediate area and that it might be weeks before they would be able to reroute one to Seker. However, there was no way that the Proctor could check his bluff, and it would give him something else to worry over. Everything would be settled in a few hours anyway, one way or the other.

"What kind of field have you used to dampen my ship's reaction pile?"

"You will have to discover that for yourself."

"Well, it makes no real difference anyway, Investigator, because if it is not stopped within two hours I will drop enough fusion bombs on Seker's surface to turn it into a black cinder."

Veblen heard the Master Magus gasp and took a deep breath before answering. "Your orbit is too close to Seker's surface for you to make that kind of foolhardy move."

An inhuman laugh rumbled through the room and the Proctor said, "I have all three of my shuttle craft using their tractor beams to pull my ship into a safe orbit; I could watch the destruction of Seker with impunity."

Veblen felt waves of despair washing away his remaining resolve. There had to be some way he could save Vera and the eggs without destroying them all! A desperate idea, incubated in the head of his distress, came alive in his mind.

"That is two hours, Investigator. Think it over."

The receiver clicked and went dead.

"We must order the 'gifted' to end their mind-control over the Proctor's ship," the Master Magus exclaimed, his voice as close to being panic stricken as Veblen had ever heard it; even when it had seemed that they would lose the docks to the Oligarch's army. "He meant what he said. He will destroy us all if we don't release his ship."

"I'm sure he does," said Veblen, "but I have a plan whereby we should be able to regain the initiative in this little war of nerves."

"What's that?" asked the Master.

"It seems to me," Veblen answered, "that if the 'gifted' can use their mindcontrol to slow down the emission of atomic particles, then they should be able to speed up that process also."

"That makes sense, but how does that help us?"

"If the 'gifted' can accelerate the movement of atomic particles in the reaction pile to where it becomes critical, then we may have more bargaining power than we had before."

"What happens if it runs out of control?"

"Then the ship and everyone aboard her will be consumed in an atomic explosion, but we'll just have to hope for the best—I don't see that we have any other alternatives."

"Do you really think that the Proctor will release Vera and the sacred eggs?"

"I don't really know," said Veblen, as a black weight seemed to press in upon his brain. The Proctors were men who had sold their humanity for a meaningless immortality in a metal shell, and there was no way he could predict how one would act. Anyone or thing which could coldly contemplate the murder of a whole planet, and its several million inhabitants, was beyond his comprehension.

"What will you do if he doesn't capitulate?"

Veblen lied. "I don't know," he answered. But deep down inside he knew. The Brotherhood had to be stopped from using the eggs as a means of expanding its malignant influence throughout the universe. He only hoped that such a decision would never have to be made.

"What are you beaming about," snapped Eral Salkow, Spokesman for the Revisionist Party. He had spent most of the last week working on an appropriations measure for the Anomian Space Navy and he was short on sleep and long on ill temper.

Advisor Armstal bent his head and eased himself into the contour seat in front of the Spokesman's desk. When the Advisor looked up, his face was set in the proper bureaucratic mask.

"Well, what is it?"

"I just heard from one of our contacts inside the Bureau of Extraterrestrial Investigations, and he told me that they had recently received a Tachyon beam from Seker."

"From Seker! What was it about?"

"It was a call for help from Investigator Veblen."

"Veblen! I thought he had been taken care of by one of your operatives. Well?"

"I had thought so too," said the Advisor slowly, "but it appears that he survived the shuttle crash unharmed."

"What shuttle crash?"

"After he survived the operative's first attempt to render him inoperative, he sabotaged the shuttle so that it would crash. . . ."

"Crash! I thought I told you that I wanted him incapacitated, not eliminated. Reliable operative . . . ha! What happened to my niece, you dunderhead!"

"Apparently, she also was able to escape from the wreckage, but Veblen claims that she has been taken prisoner by the Brotherhood."

"What is the Order of Universal Symmetry doing in all this?"

"They're the ones who gave the interplanetary spacecraft to the snake-men."

"Ophidians," corrected the Spokesman. "Poor Vera. What is he doing to rescue my niece from the Brotherhood?"

"He didn't say, Spokesman. He called to see if there were any battle cruisers in the sector."

"Were there any?"

"No, but he said that he might have to do something desperate before the Brotherhood's ship left."

"Desperate! With Vera involved? It's bad enough that your operative almost had her killed, but now *he's* going to do something desperate. If anything happens to my niece, I'm going to hold you personally responsible."

"Me!" exclaimed the Advisor. "I didn't have anything to do with her being captured. I'll admit that the operative was a little over-zealous in carrying out his duty, but I told him that Veblen was only to be temporarily put out of the way, nothing permanent. The Captain's a good man and I didn't expect him to botch the job and jeopardize Vera. But how can you blame me for what the Brotherhood has done?"

"I'm surrounded by incompetents," mumbled the Spokesman, though in truth he was more angry at himself than his assistant. After all, he had been the one responsible for arranging Vera's appointment as assistant Investigator under Thorstein Veblen. It was during times like this that he began to wonder if he had erred by placing his political goals ahead of his personal ones. There were few real friends in a politician's life, and he had never found the time for a family. Vera was the only relative of his that he was close to, and now she might possibly end up being a sacrificial pawn on his political chessboard.

"But all of this could work out very well for the party," said the Advisor, with sudden enthusiasm. "The Brotherhood has managed to capture a dozen of the Ophidian sacred eggs, and every one of those embryos has some kind of latent psychic talent. You know what that could mean?"

Yes, he knew, thought the Spokesman wearily, another threat against the Magellanics and the Protectorate that could be used as a bugaboo to coerce some of the less recalcitrant members of the Orthodoxy. For even if the Brotherhood's scientists were to learn the genetic codes that unlocked the secrets of telepathy, he knew—from long, hard experience—that this discovery would only tip the scales of galactic power temporarily. For soon, when the need arose, someone would discover a mind-shield or thought-disruptor that would restore the balance of power. Change was the universe's only constant. "Many lives will be lost," he said dully.

The Advisor droned on, oblivious of anything other than the excited torrent of thoughts racing through his mind. "The knowledge that the Brotherhood may soon possess the power of telepathy will set the Supreme Committee on the edge of their seats. This thing is even bigger than the Ophidian Rebellion. If Investigator Veblen fails, and I really don't think that he can single-handedly stop an Esoteric warship, then we'll have the majority we need. I bet we can even round up a few votes from the Reactionary Party. We will call for a vote of confidence and when the Orthodoxy fails to win a majority of the votes, we will take over the government."

"Enough of this prattle," interrupted the Spokesman, as his old political instincts began to take over. "You don't win votes by congratulating yourself. Now, first of all, I want you to contact every member of the party and explain to them what is going on—not everything, of course—and tell them to spread the news through the Senior Assembly, the Supreme Committee, and even the Inner Council."

"That is really going to stir up the opposition!"

"Set them up, is more like it," said the Spokesman, with a wicked grin.

Eighteen

THE CHIEF ENGINEER'S WORRIED face dominated the screen above the console. His voice was loud and excited. "I tell you I can't do a damn thing to stop it. The pile has gone crazy. I've put every dampening rod we have into it, and it hasn't made the least bit of difference."

"Somehow that Investigator is responsible for all of this," snarled the Proctor, his voice strained and showing signs of tension. For several seconds he debated with himself about destroying Seker, but discarded the idea since *The Sword of Wrath* was still too close to the surface of the planet to bomb it safely.

The tension in the command center was growing at the same rate as the particle bombardment in the atomic pile of the reaction drive. Several crew members jumped when the Captain's voice broke the silence. "Should I give the order to abandon ship, Proctor?"

The Proctor gave him a withering glare. "That

is not your decision to make, Captain. Must I remind you of the importance of our mission?"

For a moment it looked as though the Captain might try to defy his authority, but instead he gulped twice and began to look at the floor. The Proctor was disappointed. An abusive diatribe was just what he needed to act as a pressure valve for the tension he felt building up inside. Would the Investigator risk the life of his assistant and destroy *The Sword of Wrath?* Or was it all a bluff? Or was it possible that the Investigator had started something he could no longer control? That last question began to gnaw at his remaining patience and he began to pace around the control room.

"Look," cried the Chief Engineer, his face looming over the room. "I don't care what the rest of you do, but I'm getting the hell out of the engine room. This pile is almost ready to blow! I wouldn't give it more than two or three minutes."

"You will stay where you are until I order otherwise," commanded the Proctor, but the Chief Engineer's face disappeared and he found himself shouting at a blank screen.

"I'm not going to remain here and die like some experimental animal in a box," cried the communications officer, as he lunged out of his seat. His sentiments were reiterated by several others who began to follow him toward the control room door.

As the Proctor reached for the laser Starfire at his belt, he wondered to himself why they were so anxious to preserve their horrid little lives. Who were they to fear death, he thought with contempt, as his laser beam cleanly beheaded the navigator. The white floor turned a rich carmine as the headless torso careened around the command center, spoiling the

Proctor's aim on the communications officer who was already halfway through the opening door. He managed to jam the door mechanism with his laser fire, but more of the crew members squeezed through. After amputating the legs of one of the ship's officers, he turned off the beam in futility as the last of the crew forced their way through the half-open doorway.

Here they were running like panic-stricken animals, when it was he who had the most to lose. The almost immortal lifespan of one of the elect. There were several Proctors who had already lived over twenty thousand years, and there was no reason why they wouldn't continue living for much, much longer. No, he thought angrily, it was not right that he should die after a mere two thousand and three hundred years of life.

The Proctor began to run across the blood-splattered floor. His foot slipped on something soft and rubbery and he fell to the floor. He heard the distant roar as one of the rescue rockets was launched from its cradle.

A mindless panic took possession of his body and he scrambled to his feet. He flew through the half-opened door cutting his hand on a jagged piece of metal. The pain was barely noticeable as he raced through the maze of twisting corridors.

Someone was in his way and he tried to come to a stop. They crashed. As he started to rise to his feet, he noticed that it was the female Investigator, and she had been carrying one of the Ophidian eggs. It was now splashed all over the white wall.

"What's the matter with you," she cried.

He tried to tear himself from her grasp, but instead fell against the wall into the broken egg.

"Come with me," she ordered, as she pulled him into a nearby cabin where eight of the eggs were still cached.

"We've got to get out of here," he gibbered.

"Take one of these eggs," she said scornfully. "There's a shuttle craft waiting for me to bring some of these on board." She thrust one of the eggs into his arms, picked up one for herself, and started to walk towards the airlock.

He followed blindly.

"Can't you stop it?" Veblen cried, as he grasped one of the 'gifted' who sat in a circle on the floor, and began to shake his shoulders. The Ophidian jerked back and forth until Veblen let go and then he fell to the floor and didn't move. Two of the other 'gifted' began to scream and the young girl jumped to her feet and ran out of the room without making a sound.

"It is useless, my friend," said the Master Magus, helping Veblen to his feet. "They have lost control."

Veblen stood pensively for a moment, waiting to hear the distant thunder of an explosion, until he realized that the distance was too great for him to hear anything. Vera could have already died, her body consumed in the heart of an atomic explosion. Ice-cold slivers sliced through his veins and arteries.

"I'm sure some of them have escaped," said the Master Magus, "they had plenty of warning. I'm also sure that they would want to use Vera as a hostage."

"But they wouldn't answer when I called."

"Let's go find Haron and see if he can reestablish mindcontact with Vera."

Veblen followed as the Master led him into the

telepath's ascetic sleeping chamber.

The Master Magus woke him up and asked him to see if he could locate Vera and establish communications with her. Haron, who still looked exhausted from his last mental contact with Vera, sat up and agreed willingly. Easing himself down to the rock floor, he once again assumed the full lotus position, closed his eyes, and promptly fell into a trance.

A deep growl burst from his lips and Veblen felt himself grow weak in the knees.

"Is anything wrong?" asked the Master Magus.

"I can feel many minds full of terror and fear," replied the telepath in a listless voice.

To Veblen it seemed as though countless hours had passed before the telepath again began to speak. "She is well. There are others with her in a small skybird. The large skybird has died, its body consumed by fire and heat."

The telephath's elliptical eyes dilated and suddenly he slumped forward.

"What is it," cried Veblen, his heart battering against his chest.

"Hatred . . . fear . . . so powerful," moaned the telepath, his face twisted into a savage grimace.

"Haron," shouted Veblen, "is Vera safe? Tell me."

"She . . . is in grave danger."

Vera shook her head as though to clear her thoughts. It felt strange for her to have someone else sharing the privacy of her mind, almost as though there were little cobwebs capturing her stray thoughts. But it had helped to have some contact with Thor, even though there was little she could tell him. She was still dazed from the buffeting around the shuttle craft had received when *The Sword of*

Wrath had exploded. It was just fortunate that they hadn't been any closer to the ground.

Most of the crew members who had escaped their doomed vessel were still huddled together seeking comfort from each other. Two of them were stretched out motionless on the metal deck and there was an occasional groan from one of the others.

Vera felt something in her arms as she rose to her feet, and saw that she was still carrying one of the Ophidian eggs that she had rescued from the battle cruiser. She was surprised that it had survived the rolling and pitching the shuttle craft had been subject to, but she noticed that its shell was softer than a chicken egg and had a leathery feel to it.

She had no idea where the shuttle was headed, though she was sure they would try to land someplace on Seker. The Proctor was still standing in the same rigid stance that he had maintained throughout the voyage, even when the ship had been caught in the wake of the atomic explosion that had disintegrated *The Sword of Wrath*. She watched as his lips began to move, but no sound came out. It was eerie. One of the ship's officers began to walk toward him saying something, but she couldn't hear him either. Her ears popped and suddenly she could hear again. The moans turned to screams.

"Where should we land the shuttle, Proctor?" asked the ship's officer. "Is anything wrong? Are you all right?"

The Proctor jerked forward, as though he had just become aware of the other man's presence. He moved with an irregular motion, like that of a primitive robot. One hand darted out and grabbed the frightened officer by the throat. He began to make terrible coughing and gasping noises. Meanwhile, the Proctor

166

had stopped moving and he began to lift the dying man into the air.

He's completely crazy, thought Vera, as she tried to think of some way to help the strangling man. His face was turning a reddish purple. There were no weapons nearby and she began to scream. Everyone else was backing away from the grisly scene. "Do something!" she screamed, but no one appeared to hear her.

Then she remembered an article she had scanned sometime back, about the Esoterics; the worlds held in thrall by the Brotherhood. All the common people, or lays as they were called by the Order, were imprinted during their youth with several commands through hypno-conditioning and drugs. One of the strongest of these tenets was that they were never to harm a member of the Brotherhood. That could be the only explanation of their sheep-like acquiescence as he killed one of their number.

The officer was no longer thrashing around and the Proctor let him drop with a thud. Then the Proctor's hand began to jerk down towards the laser Starfire hooked on his belt.

Vera felt the blood pounding against her temples and her mouth was dry as desert sand. The Proctor grasped the Starfire's handle and he began to aim it toward the panic-stricken crew members. Vera looked for something to throw and remembered the egg cradled in her arms. A re-entry alarm began to make its warning cry. Vera knew that the egg she held was fertile and contained a young Ophidian life. The Starfire was now pointing right into the center of the screaming crew members. Did she have the right to sacrifice the life she held in her arms; yet, hadn't one of the crew members released her from her cabin aboard *The Sword of Wrath,* thereby saving her from certain death. She stood there frozen as the Proctor's thumb moved towards the firing stud.

"I've failed. I've failed!" shrieked the Proctor in a staccato scream. He began to fire the laser.

Vera saw an explosion of red and she threw the egg. It knocked the laser out of the Proctor's hand and there was a fountain of sparks and fire as the laser's beam struck the equipment panel. Dense black smoke poured through the room, and she had to strain her eyes to see him. She shoved her way through the writhing bodies until she found one of the senior crew members. He was dead. The top of his head, right above his eyebrows, had been removed just like the lid off a canister. She felt her stomach begin to heave, but forced the vile fluid back down her throat. Finding the officer's laser, she looked up to see the Proctor standing above her with his hands reaching for her throat.

She whipped the laser up, aimed it at the Proctor's chest, and pressed the firing stud. A cloudburst of blood poured down upon her and the odor of burning flesh seared her nostrils. It left her gagging, but she was still alive.

Looking down at the scattered dead and wounded, she shook her head in dismay. Then she heard the clamor of the re-entry warning. There was no time for remorse or sorrow. Turning away from the gore-splattered deck, she searched for a senior officer. She found one dazed but still alive. In curt and no-nonsense terms, she told him to change the ship's course and head for Buzthara. As he ran towards the control console, she noticed that she still held the laser in her hand. She tucked it into her belt, since it was obvious that the demoralized crew would follow anyone who gave them orders. While the officer changed course, she checked the damages. All the communications equipment was dead, along with the autopilot, but the shuttle could still fly and Vera felt that was more than enough to be thankful for.

Nineteen

THE INDIGO-COLORED WAITER escorted Veblen, Vera, and the Master Magus to a table facing a glass aquarium which ran the length of the room. This was the first time Veblen had ever entered an Ophidian restaurant and he felt a little uneasy. However, his worries about ordering were ended when the dark blue waiter asked, "Floutee?"

"That will be fine," said the Master Magus, who then turned to his guests and added, "the house specialty. I hope you don't mind my ordering for you?"

"Not at all," said Veblen, as he watched one of the flatcake-shaped fish swim the length of the tank.

The waiter returned moments later with a tray bearing three small glasses filled with an amber liquid.

"Let me warn you both," said the Master Magus, "Sool is a very potent drink, so take your time drinking it."

Veblen took a small sip and felt a rivulet of Greek fire run down to his stomach. He looked at Vera

170

and saw her eyes widen as she quickly set down the rest of her drink. After giving her a sympathetic smile, he squeezed her hand.

"Sool derives its distinctive taste from the three different mushrooms that are added after the grains have fermented. It is only properly aged after no less than twenty years."

Veblen took another small swallow and noticed a slight tang in his mouth, deciding that he would have to take the Ophidian's word for it. "Let me propose a toast," said Veblen, holding his glass out before him. "To the new First Elder and may his reign end more successfully than that of his predecessor."

Veblen and Vera laughed and the new First Elder gave him a wry grin. "It is really only an interim position," said the Master Magus, "because I will only hold the position until next spring when the Bitis Tribe takes over clan leadership. But I think it will help us to formalize some of the university's positions."

"Formalize!" said Veblen. "Isn't that a mild way to describe your Proclamation of Human Equal Rights?"

"Well," the Master Magus said, with a smile, "you must admit that the majority of Buzthara's anti-humans are no longer with us, and that the political climate is right for such a proclamation. After all, it is quite obvious that without the help of the city's human population and the Thadrons, the planet would be headed for disaster."

Veblen watched as the Ophidian waiter leaned over the aquarium and held his hand several centimeters above the water's surface.

"What is the waiter doing?" asked Vera.

Without turning his head to look, the Master Magus

said, "He's catching our dinner."

"Our dinner!"

"Yes, Floutee is raw fish served with ranswr sauce. It is considered to be a delicacy. As with any fish, the sooner it is eaten the better it tastes. One of the major reasons most fish has such a distinctive fishy taste is that it has a tendency to rapidly decompose right after it has been killed. You will not find any fresher fish than that served here."

Veblen watched as the waiter's hand snaked down into the tank and grasped a squirming fish. Seconds later, he slapped it down on a flat table and picked up a long-bladed knife. Then he carefully filleted the still-breathing fish. When this was finished, he threw the remains of the fish in a bucket and returned to the tank. Veblen's stomach was beginning to feel a bit queasy so he turned away. While he had eaten far stranger dishes than raw fish during his stay in the Bureau, he hadn't always watched their preparation.

A few minutes later the waiter brought several small dishes containing a pale pink sauce, and then their plates with the fish fillets. Veblen gave Vera a brave smile and then he picked up a piece of fish and dunked it into the sauce. In spite of the revulsion he had felt earlier, he discovered that the Floutee was delicious, and his estimation of Ophidian cuisine went up considerably.

"How much longer will the two of you be staying on Seker?"

"The Bureau told me that they would have a survey craft in this sector in about three standard months, so Vera and I will be on a vacation of sorts until then."

The Master Magus said, "I'm glad to hear it, maybe

it will give us a chance to pay back a little of what we owe the both of you for what you have done. In fact, we were planning a large reception. . . ."

Veblen interrupted. "It's not that we don't appreciate what you're trying to do, Elder." He paused, looked at Vera, and then continued when she nodded her head. "It's just that what the two of us want most right now is a little privacy . . . I think you understand?"

He smiled and said, "Of course, and may I offer my congratulations. After all you both have been through, you deserve some time together—alone."

"You can say that again," said Veblen, with a hungry smile.

"However," said the Master Magus, "I would like to take this opportunity, on the behalf of my people, to thank you both again for saving Seker from certain disaster. Now don't try and deny it," he added, before Veblen or Vera could protest. "Furthermore, Vera, we appreciate your efforts to save the sacred eggs."

"I'm sorry that I was only able to rescue three of them, but time was running out and. . . ."

"Don't belittle your accomplishments, Vera, because, truthfully, we never expected to see any of them again. Besides, there shall be more eggs this year," he concluded, giving them both a conspiratorial wink.

The two of them blushed and Veblen quickly said, "Now don't get the wrong idea, we haven't decided to apply for a permanent bonding, although. . . . ," he looked at Vera and they both turned a deep shade of scarlet.

"I understand," said the Master Magus. "Don't forget that I too was once young."

The waiter returned with more Sool and they all made a toast to the future. "In case I don't have the opportunity again," said the Master Magus, "I'd like to extend a personal invitation to the two of you to feel free to return to Seker any time that either of you has the opportunity."

"That might prove difficult, Elder, because of Seker's non-contact status, but I'm going to do everything I can to see that classification changed. I would like to see Seker offered League membership."

"Is that possible?"

"Technically, you meet all the membership qualifications," said Veblen.

"He's right," added Vera. Not only have you learned of the League's existence, but now you have several interplanetary spacecraft, and that means you qualify as a space-faring culture."

"But we didn't develop them ourselves."

"There are loopholes in any charter," said Vera, "and you can count on Thor to find a way to thread the loop." They both exchanged a quick grin and then she continued. "Furthermore, I have an uncle who holds a high position in our government, who may be able to help . . . that is, if he can ever forgive me for joining forces with the enemy."

"What's wrong?" asked Spokesman Salkow, as his white-faced Advisor walked into his office.

"We're ruined," he muttered.

"Speak up, man."

"We're going to be laughed right out of the Supreme Committee."

"What is going on?" demanded the Spokesman.

"I just received word from our contact in the Bureau, that the Director received another Tachyon message from the planet Seker."

"He did! Well, go on."

"Somehow Investigator Veblen managed to foil the Brotherhood's plans and destroy their battle cruiser."

"What about my niece?" asked the Spokesman anxiously; political losses could be taken, absorbed, but lately, he had begun to realize that Vera occupied a unique place in his heart—one that could not be replaced.

"Apparently, Spokesman, she managed to escape from the Brotherhood's ship and then, somehow—I didn't get all the details, killed the Proctor and took command of the escaping craft . . . but, damn it, that's not important. We made promises to people and after word of this gets out we'll be the laughing stock of the Committee for a long time to come."

The Spokesman broke into a big smile. He should have known better than to have worried about Vera. She was too much like himself to have been taken care of that easily.

"This will put the party back years. . . ."

"Not necessarily," interrupted the Spokesman. "There's always a way to make political coin out of anything, even a disaster." He paused to give the Advisor a hard glare, and then continued, "If you don't succumb to panic first."

"But what do you suggest?"

"In this case, I think a quick offensive blow is called for, before our opponents have time to take advantage of our miscalculation. I want you to contact our party leaders and tell them that we have changed positions on the Seker situation. Tell them that it is time we welcomed the Ophidians into the Anomian League."

"What!" stammered the Advisor. "But they'll never

qualify for membership in the league. . . ."

"They have spacecraft. Right?"

"Yes, but. . . ."

"They have a unified planetary government. Right?"

"Yes," sputtered Advisor Armstal, "but they keep humans as slaves."

"I have no doubt that if we offer them League membership, with all its obvious benefits, that it can all be worked out."

"But the Ophidians aren't even human!"

"Good," said the Spokesman. "When the Orthodoxy begins to scream about all of this, we will accuse them of non-human prejudice."

"You can't be serious!"

"Enough of your chatter," stormed the Spokesman. "Contact the party leaders at once and give them all the necessary information. I want to spring this on the Orthodoxy before they even realize what has happened."

As the Advisor walked out in stunned silence, Spokesman Eral Salkow wondered what Vera would think about all this when she returned from Seker. She'll adjust, he thought, after he explained it to her, she would understand. And Investigator Veblen, he might even become a member of the Revisionist Party after spending a couple of months with Vera. He chuckled to himself for several minutes.

THE END